# THE CHILDREN'S
# ATLAS OF
# EXPLORATION

# THE CHILDREN'S ATLAS OF EXPLORATION

## FOLLOW IN THE FOOTSTEPS OF THE GREAT EXPLORERS

### ANTONY MASON

The Millbrook Press
Brookfield, Ct.

A QUARTO BOOK

First published in the United States of America in 1993 by
The Millbrook Press Inc.
2 Old New Milford Road
Brookfield, Connecticut 06804.

**Library of Congress Cataloging-in-Publication Data**

Mason, Antony.
    The children's atlas of exploration/by Antony Mason and Keith Lye.
    p.   cm.
    Includes index.
    Summary: An atlas depicting exploration through the ages, from the wanderings of
prehistoric peoples to modern space missions.
    ISBN 1-56294-711-7 (trade ed.),   ISBN 1-56294-256-5 (lib. ed.), ISBN 1-56294-925-X (club ed.)
    1. Discoveries in geography--Maps.      2. Voyages and travels--Maps.
3. Explorers--History--Maps.
[1. Discoveries in geography--Maps.      2. Voyages and travels--Maps.      3. Explorers--Maps.
4. Atlases.]
I. Lye, Keith.   II. Title   III. Title: Atlas of exploration
G1036.M3   1993  <G&M>
911--dc20                                                            92-28856
                                                                          CIP
                                                                       MAP AC


This book was designed and produced by
Quarto Publishing plc
The Old Brewery, 6 Blundell Street, London N7 9BH

**Consultant** Keith Lye
**Creative Director** Nick Buzzard
**Senior Editor** Cynthia O'Brien
**Editor** Michael Johnstone
**Designer** Martin Lovelock
**Design Assistant** Trish Going
**Maps** Janos Marffy
**Illustrator** Jim Robins
**Picture Research** Liz Eddison


The Publishers would like to thank the following for
their help in the preparation of this book: Malcolm
Porter (Contour), Ben Goold, Susan Millership, Karen Ball.

Typeset by Proteus Typesetters, Worle, England
Manufactured by Eray Scan Pte Ltd, Singapore
Printed by Star Standard (Pte) Ltd, Singapore

# CONTENTS

Exploration is as old as the human race. Natural curiosity has always driven people to discover what lies beyond the existing limits of their knowledge about the world. Exploration has taken many different forms, and it is not always easy to say who is an explorer.

## THE NEED TO EXPLORE

Curiosity is one of the great driving forces of human life. Over the last 100,000 years or so, the human race has been repeatedly asking the questions "How?" and "Why?" Throughout the ages, curiosity about the surrounding world has tempted people to explore — to find out what lies beyond the part of the world that they already know.

The nature of exploration has changed over time. Early human beings went out in search of better hunting grounds and safe places to live. The first farmers looked for fertile valleys where there was a reliable supply of water. Traders traveled to new lands to find new customers for their wares and to look for new goods to sell at home.

When the ancient civilizations of Mesopotamia, China, Egypt, and Greece began to develop a respect for learning and knowledge, this led to a new kind of exploration: the search for knowledge for its own sake. Travelers would set out to find the answers to questions that intrigued them. What lay beyond those mountains? Where did this river begin? Where did that river reach the sea? There was only one way to find out, and that was to travel into the unknown, which has always required courage and daring.

**Below** Many explorers went in search of new lands to settle. Some communities, such as this one of rice farmers in Borneo, have never settled, but use small areas of land until these are exhausted.

**Right** In the pursuit of knowledge about the world, geographers and mapmakers have to piece together all the information brought home by travelers, traders, and explorers.

## Mapping the world

From the 15th century on, European explorers realized the value of good maps. They took great care to make them accurate, as the coast of this 16th-century map of South America shows. By the 18th century, the desire to map the whole world was paramount.

**Below** Some early maps of the world are basically images which reflect a religion or philosophy. In this 13th-century French map, much of the northern hemisphere is occupied by Christian countries of the Mediterranean. Zodiac signs straddle the Equator.

**Above** Rumors, myths, and tall tales about monsters and strange occurrences in remote lands and oceans made the idea of distant travel seem doubly dangerous to early explorers. Illustrations such as this one, dated 1539, offered little comfort. Such pictures may have been based on genuine reports by travelers, but it is difficult to describe any animal from memory to someone who has never seen it.

### Forgotten heroes

Until recent centuries, very little exploration was carried out for the sake of knowledge alone. Marco Polo (pictured here with his caravan of camels on a map made in 1375) set out on his 24-year voyage to China and the Far East in the hope of becoming rich by trade. He became famous mainly because he told of his adventures in a book, although only a few people read it at the time. But if it had not been for his chance meeting with a writer during a three-year spell as a prisoner of war in Genoa, this book might never have been written.

Numerous navigators, travelers, and traders have been forgotten because they did not leave records of their voyages. For example, over 3,000 years ago the Polynesian navigators sailed vast distances across the Pacific Ocean in their flimsy outrigger boats in search of new lands, yet their achievements are only vaguely remembered in myths. In many such cases, records were not needed at the time; in others, the records have been lost; and in the case of some, their discoveries were deliberately kept secret so that rival traders or nations would not profit from their efforts.

# THE REAL EXPLORERS

The classic image of the true explorer is a person traveling in great hardship through uncharted lands, patiently making maps and keeping records of everything observed — the land, people, animals, and plants — while fighting off life-threatening diseases, dangerous animals, and hostile natives. But exploration can take many forms, and who really deserves to be given the title of explorer is often hard to say.

It is easier to recognize those who are clearly not explorers. Tourists, for example, may travel to remote places, but they are not explorers. Conquering generals are not usually thought to be explorers — yet sometimes they were accompanied by surveyors and mapmakers who did explore and find out more about the lands they invaded. Traveling to an unknown country and staying there is not exploration either. People who do this are thought of as settlers, not explorers, although some inquisitive settlers who ventured beyond these settlements to see what they could discover can be considered explorers.

To take all such problems into account, the definition of an explorer has to remain rather vague. Thus, an explorer is someone who travels to places which are previously unknown to his or her people, gathers and records knowledge about these places, and then takes or sends this knowledge back home.

## Discovery

It is often claimed that explorers *discover* new lands. For example, it used to be said that Christopher Columbus discovered the Americas when he sailed across the Atlantic to the Caribbean Islands in the *Santa Maria* (above) in 1492. The word "discover" is misleading. These islands were already inhabited by Arawaks and Caribs.

Columbus found places about which he — and the rest of Europe — previously knew nothing. It was a discovery only from the European point of view. The fact that he went on to rename many of the islands, and to claim them for Spain, was typical of the behavior of European explorers during the 15th and 16th centuries. Such arrogance and aggression has given the term "discovery" a bad name.

**Left** Some of the early explorers were ruthless and greedy, particularly in the case of many of the Spanish in Central and South America.

**Below** Explorers travel to improve our knowledge of the world. Anthropologists study people such as these Ika Indians in Colombia.

**Above** European exploration changed in the 18th century when the thirst for trade and territory began to be replaced by the more gentle pursuits of geography and science. The French explorer La Pérouse, here seen on Easter Island, was an example of this new, less aggressive type of explorer.

**Right** *Skylab 1* marked an important step in the new dimension for exploration: space. Although it involves a level of technology quite unknown in previous eras, space travel has many aspects in common with the best time-honored traditions of exploration.

## The world is a jigsaw puzzle

Each community in the world builds up its own knowledge about the world. For example, a European's understanding of the world is quite different from that of a Tuareg nomad in the Sahara Desert. We cannot say that one is better than the other. The Tuaregs' knowledge of the Sahara is far more useful to them than the Europeans' idea of the world would be.

The world is like a jigsaw puzzle. Each piece is a different community that has its own view of the world and its own knowledge about it. Likewise each community has its own explorers, who travel into other pieces of the jigsaw and bring back knowledge of them. The information that is gained helps them to see how neighboring pieces fit in with their own. The ultimate goal has always been to complete the jigsaw.

Explorers, traders, settlers, conquerors, and missionaries have all played their part in mapping Europe. Tribes and nations have jostled each other for territory and dominance, and in the 15th century this restless urge stimulated Europeans into venturing overseas.

# EARLY CIVILIZATIONS

Human beings arrived in Europe some 100,000 years ago, probably from northern Africa, and began spreading north about 11,000 years ago.

The earliest European civilizations developed in the eastern Mediterranean from around 2000 BC with the Minoans (centering on the island of Crete) and the Mycenaeans (on mainland Greece). The city-states of ancient Greece developed from around 1000 BC. By about 750 BC both the Greeks and the Phoenicians had explored much of the Mediterranean and created trading colonies.

The ancient Greek civilization was the first in Europe to attempt to analyze the world in a scientific way. Geographers and astronomers used observation, and information from travelers, to make maps of the Mediterranean and the world.

**Below** The Greek-Egyptian astronomer Ptolemy worked in the Library of Alexandria from AD 127 to 150. He brought together all of Greek learning about geography to produce a world map. It remained the best world map until the 15th century. The original is lost.

**Above** The Phoenicians were master shipbuilders and the greatest traders of the Mediterranean. This relief carving made in 702 BC shows a Phoenician galley. By this time the Phoenicians had established colonies throughout the Mediterranean.

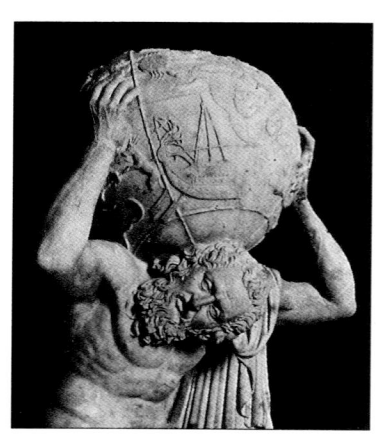

**Above** The Greek god Atlas is often portrayed carrying the world on his shoulders. Although there were many theories about the shape of the Earth, around 200 BC the mathematician Eratosthenes calculated the circumference of the world, and miscalculated by just 155 miles (250 km).

## The ends of the world

According to the ancient Greeks, Hercules created the headlands at either side of the Strait of Gibraltar during his tenth labor, when he had to obtain the oxen of the monster Geryon from Erythia.

For many years the Greeks regarded the Pillars of Hercules as the eastern extremity of their world. Beyond them lay the world's edge.

Between 310 and 306 BC, the Greek explorer Pytheas of Marseilles sailed through the Pillars, up the Atlantic coast of what is now Portugal and, it is said, circumnavigated Britain before sailing for home. Pytheas sailed not for trading reasons, but out of real scientific interest.

**Left** Some people believe that Pytheas of Marseilles may have visited the Faroe Islands in the north Atlantic on his voyage of exploration that extended the Greeks' knowledge of the world beyond the Mediterranean.

**Below** Human development in Europe generally followed a northward direction after the first inhabitants spread out from Asia and Africa. Farming and town-dwelling civilizations spread north from their early centers in the eastern Mediterranean.

NORTH SEA

Scandinavian ice sheet

Ice sheet withdrew 11,000-10,000 years ago

Limit of human occupation 100,000-40,000 years ago

Human migration 100,000-40,000 years ago

Limit of human occupation to 100,000 years ago

ATLANTIC OCEAN

Danube

Human migration 100,000-40,000 years ago

Human migration 100,000-40,000 years ago

BLACK SEA

CASPIAN SEA

Marseilles

MEDITERRANEAN SEA

Mycenae GREECE

ASIA MINOR

CRETE

Tigris

PHOENICIA

Euphrates

Strait of Gibraltar

THE GULF

AFRICA

Alexandria (founded 332 BC)

Early human migration

Nile

RED SEA

■ Under Phoenician influence

▨ Mycenaean world (c.1300 BC)

■ Under Greek influence (c.750 BC)

# THE ROMAN WORLD

The Romans continued to expand on the knowledge of the world that the Greeks had established. But their intentions were rather different. The work of the Roman mapmakers and surveyors was essentially about creating and maintaining an empire.

At its largest, the Roman Empire included all the lands bordering the Mediterranean, east as far as Mesopotamia (modern Iraq), and all of western Europe as far north as Britain, where Hadrian's Wall marked the northern-most extent of their conquests.

The Romans also knew about India from the campaigns of Alexander the Great (see pages 24–25), and they had some idea about the Far East because trade goods from China reached the Roman world by way of the Silk Road (see pages 22–23). Nonetheless, they rarely ventured beyond their own boundaries.

The Romans did, however, travel extensively within the Empire. Both the ancient Greeks and Romans produced books and travel guides for sightseers. A famous example of this is *Hellados Periegesis* ("Guided Tour of Greece"), written in the 2nd century AD by the Greek author Pausanias.

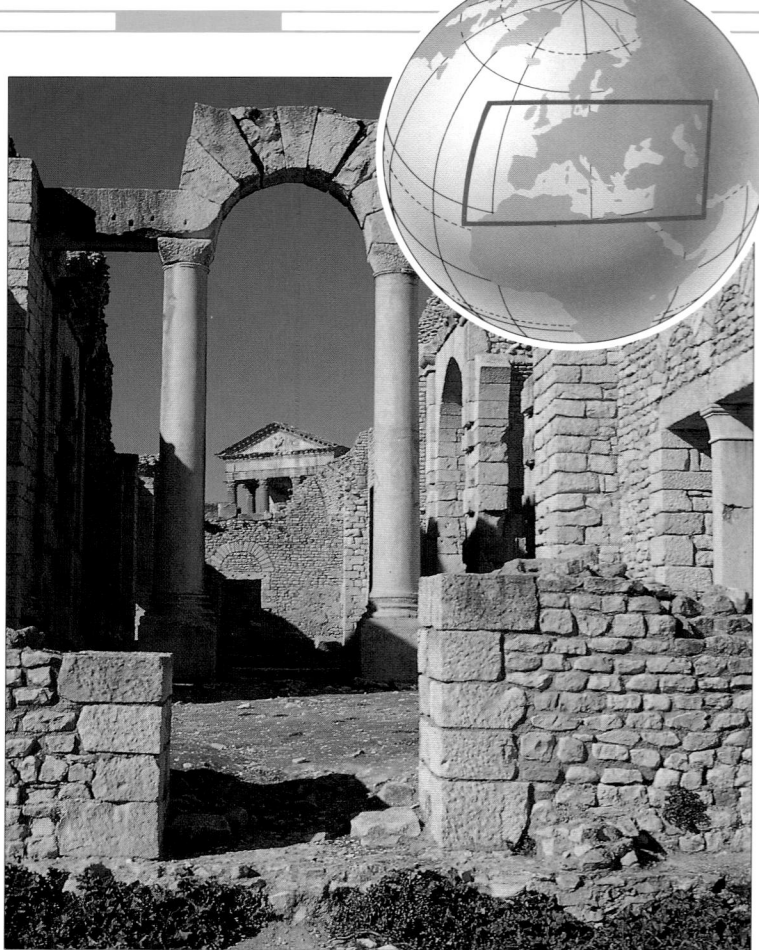

**Above** The Romans conquered what they called "Africa" (modern Tunisia) in the 2nd century BC, and built Dougga on the site of an old Phoenician city. As a way of expressing their power over conquered lands, the Romans liked to build monuments on a grand scale, even in the most remote corners of their Empire.

**Right** The Roman Empire reached its height in the 2nd century AD, when the Romans controlled the entire Mediterranean, as well as all neighboring countries — which they occupied in order to protect the Mediterranean. The conquest of Britain was an exception to this general strategy.

### All roads lead to Rome

The Romans were great road-builders, because they knew that they had to have good communications in order to rule their Empire effectively. The shortest distance between two points is a straight line, so they built their roads as straight as possible to make the quickest routes for sending supplies and messengers — and armies in case of trouble. Even today in many parts of Europe, modern roads follow the same routes taken by the old Roman roads. You can often recognize such roads because they are so straight and because they continue for such extraordinarily long distances.

Maps were made of these roads for the use of the administrators and generals. The "Table of Peutinger" (above) is a 22.3 ft (6.8 m) long map which shows the Roman Empire in a simplified form. It marks roads and the distances between towns.

The "Table of Peutinger" is probably a 13th-century copy of an original made in the 3rd or 4th century AD. It was discovered in Germany in the 15th century and is named after Konrad Peutinger, who owned it after 1507.

**Right** Hadrian's Wall marked the most northerly limit of the Roman Empire (below). The wall stretched some 74 miles (120 km) across northern England, almost from coast to coast, and was built under orders from Emperor Hadrian in the 120s and 130s AD.

**Map labels:**

HIBERNIA

BRITANNIA

Hadrian's Wall

NORTH SEA (MARE GERMANICUM)

Rhine

GERMANIA

BELGICA

LUGDUNENSIS

Danube

ATLANTIC OCEAN (OCEANUS ATLANTICUS)

AQUITANIA

Rhône

DACIA

NARBONENSIS

• Pont du Gard

ILLYRICUM

I T A L I A

Rome (Roma)

TARRACONENSIS

LUSITANIA

BLACK SEA (PONTUS EUXINUS)

THRACIA

BITHYNIA PONTUS

GALATIA CAPPADOCIA

ARMENIA

A S I A

BAETICA

Carthage

Dougga

CILICIA

SYRIA

MESOPOTAMIA

CASPIAN SEA (MARE CASPIUM)

MAURETANIA

NUMIDIA

MEDITERRANEAN SEA (MARE INTERNUM)

PHOENICIA

JUDAEA

Tigris

Euphrates

A F R I C A

ARABIA

THE GULF (SINUS PERSICUS)

A E G Y P T U S

Nile

RED SEA (SINUS ARABICUS)

Extent of Roman Empire, AD 116

**Below** The Pont du Gard in the south of France was built as an aqueduct in the 1st century BC. It shows engineering skills that remained unmatched for hundreds of years after the Roman Empire collapsed.

## Masters of the seas

Until the 3rd century BC the Phoenicians possessed the finest fleet in the Mediterranean. The Romans learned the secrets of Phoenician ship design by studying a wreck. They took control of the sea and of trade throughout the Mediterranean in 260 BC during the first war against the powerful Phoenician colony of Carthage. This wall painting shows grain being loaded onto a merchant ship at Ostia, the port of Rome. Goods could be moved quite quickly as a Roman cargo ship such as this could travel about 100 miles (160 km) a day. The men who rowed were galley slaves, often the citizens of conquered lands who were dragooned into the galleys.

# BARBARIANS AND MISSIONARIES

The Roman Empire was already in decline by the 5th century AD when a series of attacks by fearsome armies from eastern Europe brought it to its knees. By AD 476 the old Roman Empire had collapsed. However, the first Christian emperor of Rome, Constantine I, who ruled from AD 306 to 337, had founded Constantinople (now Istanbul in modern Turkey), and this became the center of the Christian Byzantine Empire which lasted until the 15th century.

Much of the learning of the ancient, classical world was lost in this turbulent period, and even more was lost over the following centuries. The Christian Church remained the main source of learning in Europe for at least the next 1,000 years.

Some of the great travelers of these centuries were Christian missionaries, who set out to spread the Gospel to the pagan tribes that occupied much of the old Roman Empire. Although it had never become a Roman territory, Ireland was converted to Christianity after about AD 440. A number of missionaries traveled from there to take Christianity to the peoples of continental Europe. St. Brendan may even have reached America.

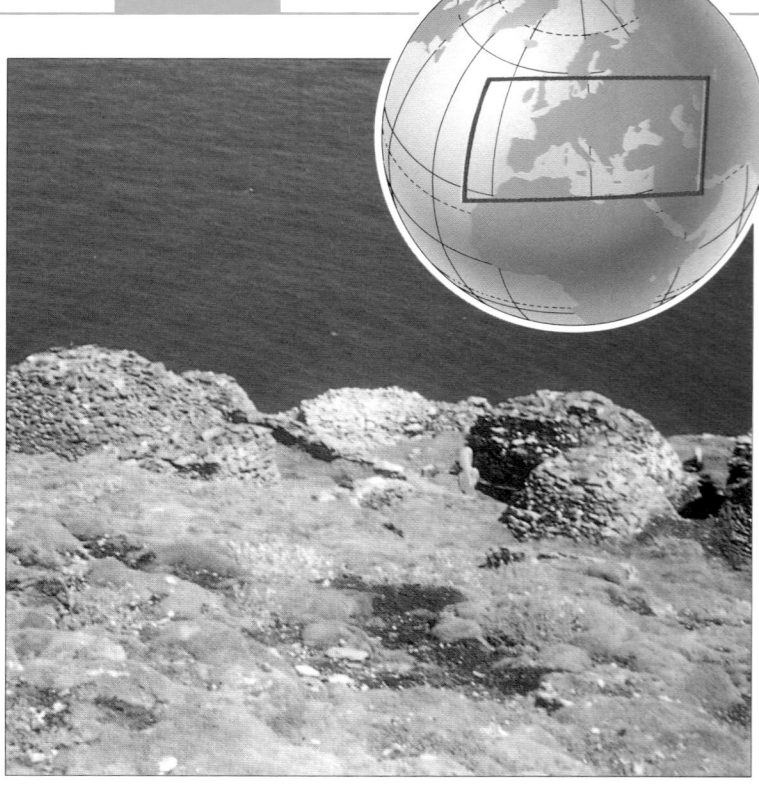

**Above** Many early Christians lived as hermits, shutting themselves away from the world and devoting their lives to prayer and contemplation. These very simple stone huts, known as *clochans* or beehive cells, were built by Irish Christians in about AD 800.

**Below** The Visigoths, led by King Alaric I, destroyed Rome in AD 410, as shown in this painting. They later conquered Roman provinces in Spain and Gaul. The Vandals took Roman North Africa in AD 429. Italy was attacked by the Huns in AD 452.

### The original Vandals

The collapse of the Roman Empire can be traced back to about AD 370 when the Huns of central Asia began attacking the Germanic tribes of eastern Europe, such as the Vandals and Goths, who in turn attacked the Romans to the west. These peoples were known to the Romans as "barbarians," which meant "uncivilized and foreign." In AD 476, Odovacar led his vast Barbarian army into Italy, took over, and declared himself king. Barbarians now controlled the western Roman Empire.

**Left** A granite high cross at Castledermot, County Kildare, dating from the 9th century AD, shows the distinctive intertwining patterns of Irish Celtic art. This can also be seen on their jewelery and church treasures. Despite repeated attacks by the Vikings (see pages 16–17), for about 400 years the monasteries of Ireland provided one of the great centers for learning, art, and culture in Europe.

**Below** The Huns, Goths, and Vandals had taken over most of the Roman world by the end of the 5th century AD. In the following centuries Christianity spread out from its main centers in Rome and Constantinople (now Istanbul), as well as from Ireland.

## Was it America?

St. Brendan (about AD 484–577) was one of the major figures of the early Irish Church and founded a number of important monasteries. He was also a great traveler, and is the hero of a saga called *Navigatio Sancti Brendani* which was translated into several European languages. This describes his seven-year sea-voyage, accompanied by 12 disciples, in which he discovers the "Land Promised to Saints." It is widely believed that the story is based on a true voyage, and that St. Brendan may even have reached America.

→ Expansion of Christianity, 6th — 9th centuries

→ Monastic expansion from Ireland

Areas under control of Germanic invaders in AD 493

 Ostrogoths

 Burgundians

Franks

Visigoths

Vandals

NORTH SEA

BALTIC SEA

Picts

Angles

IRELAND

BRITAIN

Celts

Saxons

Saxons

Slavs

Huns 451

Celts

Frisians

Rhine

FRANKISH KINGDOM

Huns c. 370

ATLANTIC OCEAN

Celts

AQUITANIA

KINGDOM OF BURGUNDY

Lombards

Huns 452

OSTROGOTHIC KINGDOM

Danube

Huns

Sueves

Basques

VISIGOTHIC KINGDOM

Rome

447 443

BLACK SEA

Constantinople

ASIA MINOR

Carthage

Vandals

MEDITERRANEAN SEA

AFRICA

# VIKING TRAVELERS

For three centuries after AD 800 the sight of a Viking warship would bring terror to the towns and villages that lined the coasts of western Europe. The Vikings were ruthless raiders. They came to steal food, cattle, and treasure from the churches and monasteries, and to capture strong and healthy young men and women to sell as slaves.

The Vikings came from the lands now known as Norway, Sweden, and Denmark. Although they are remembered mainly as raiders, they were also settlers and traders. By the 11th century there were Viking settlements across northern Europe from Russia to Ireland. Trading expeditions took them as far as the Mediterranean Sea and down the River Volga to the Caspian Sea.

They settled in Iceland from around AD 870. In about AD 986 Erik the Red, an adventurer who had been banished from Norway for murder, sailed on from Iceland to found the Eastern Settlement, a colony in Greenland around Brattahlid.

Fourteen years later, Erik the Red's son, Leif Eriksson, set off on a voyage of exploration and found three new lands which he named Helluland, Markland, and Vinland.

The true location of Vinland could only be guessed at until the 1960s when the remains of a Viking settlement were found on the coast of Newfoundland, showing that the Vikings were probably the first Europeans to reach the Americas.

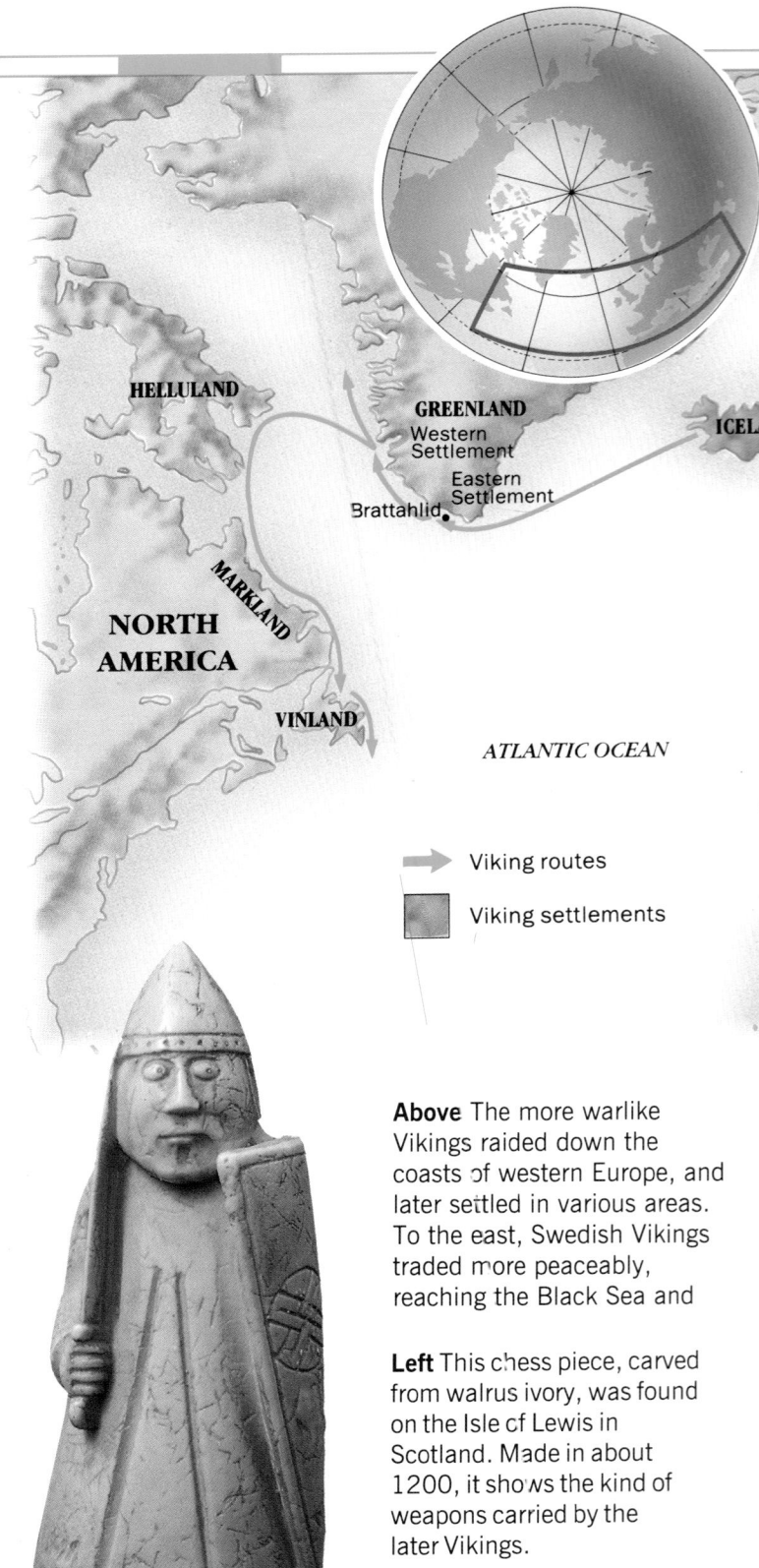

**Above** The more warlike Vikings raided down the coasts of western Europe, and later settled in various areas. To the east, Swedish Vikings traded more peaceably, reaching the Black Sea and

**Left** This chess piece, carved from walrus ivory, was found on the Isle of Lewis in Scotland. Made in about 1200, it shows the kind of weapons carried by the later Vikings.

**Left** This memorial stone from Gotland, Sweden, shows the delicate quality of Viking craftsmanship. The lower part illustrates a Viking warship. The upper part shows a warrior approaching Valhalla, where Viking heros were said to go after death in battle.

**Right** In Iceland the Vikings found a landscape similar to the rocky fjords of their homelands. The search for new and better farming land to feed an increasing population may have been one reason why the Vikings began raiding.

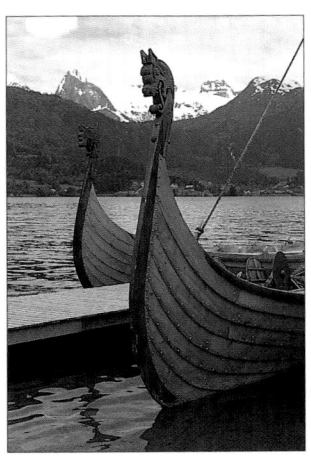

SCANDINAVIA

Norwegians

Swedes

SHETLAND ISLANDS

NORTH SEA

Danes

BALTIC SEA

• Novgorod

RITAIN

K I E V A N

• Kiev

R U S S I A

Volga

ITALY

Constantinople

BLACK SEA

CASPIAN SEA

BYZANTINE EMPIRE

MEDITERRANEAN SEA

## NORTH AFRICA

the Caspian Sea, where they came into contact with the Arab world. Western expeditions to Iceland, Greenland, and North America were carried out by settlers in search of land.

**Right** The monks in Ireland built massive "round towers" in which to hide from Viking raiders. The stone walls were more than 6 feet (2 m) thick at the base. The monks used a ladder to reach the entrance, which was set at least 13 feet (4 m) off the ground.

## Longships and knorrs

From the 8th to the 11th century AD, the Vikings were the most skilled boatbuilders and seamen in northern Europe. Their raiding parties used longships of up to 92 feet (28 m) in length, driven by a single rectangular sail and 16 pairs of oars.

Longships were built of overlapping planks of wood and were double-ended: the stern looked the same as the bow. They were steered by an oar called a *steerboard* fixed to one side (hence our term starboard).

Cargo ships, called *knorrs*, were constructed in a similar way but tended to be much wider. The Vikings may have made their journeys across the Atlantic in *knorrs*.

## Viking treasure

Collections of Viking treasures have been discovered all over Europe. Not all of these had been stolen. The Vikings were gifted craftsmen and made beautiful jewelery for themselves, while the large hoards of silver coins could well have been the profits from successful trading ventures. The presence of Arab coins in a treasure hoard found in Sweden (right) demonstrates that their trading links extended at least as far as the Middle East.

# THE RENAISSANCE AND EUROPEAN EXPANSION

Toward the end of the medieval period, from the 5th to the 15th century, there was a gradual change of mood in Europe that has become known as the Renaissance, or "rebirth." It was inspired by a new appreciation of the achievements of the ancient Greeks and Romans. The Renaissance brought fresh ideas to all areas of learning.

"Renaissance men" represented the spirit of the age. They enjoyed using any talent they might possess and led energetic lives as artists, poets, scholars, politicians, soldiers, and adventurers, often sponsored by enlightened European monarchs.

When such people looked at the maps of the time, they saw just how much remained to be discovered. Very little was known about Africa or Asia, except that these were the sources of gold, spices, silk, and precious stones. Previously these goods had been traded across the Mediterranean by middlemen, such as the Arabs, but few Europeans knew what lay beyond the Mediterranean ports.

In the 15th century, European traders and adventurers set out to discover the way to the East. By the end of the century they had reached India and the Americas; by 1522 they had traveled right around the world.

**Above** Because medieval mapmakers often invented geography so as to present an image of the world that reflected Christian teaching (for example, they might start by placing Jerusalem at the center), navigators in the 15th century used maps first made by the Greeks and Romans.

**Below** The Belem Tower, built in 1515, stands beside the River Tagus in Lisbon, Portugal. Many explorers passed beneath its walls on their way to new worlds in Africa, the Far East, and South America. Within a few years similar fortresses had been built around the world.

## The tools of exploration

A variety of navigational instruments came into general use during the 15th century, such as the compass, dividers, hourglass, star charts, and tables, which all became part of the navigator's kit. The backstaff was used to measure the angle of the sun, from which a ship's latitude could be calculated. With such instruments, navigators could work out their precise position and chart their voyages accurately.

**Below** Although many peoples sent out expeditions to explore the world, it was the Europeans who were the first to attempt to explore the world systematically. Spreading out from their home ports, they reached most of the coastal regions of the world in less than a century.

### A ship for explorers

The Portuguese *caravel* was well suited to exploration. At about 69 feet (21 m) in length, it was small by modern standards, and could be sailed by a crew of 20. It had a distinctive shape with a high "poop" deck at the stern for the helmsman and navigator, and an equally high deck at the bow. However, the breadth of the ship (nearly 25 feet [7.5 m]) and the rounded shape of the hull made it stable in heavy seas. As well as ordinary square sails, it also had triangular sails, a combination that greatly improved maneuverability in winds.

GREENLAND — ARCTIC OCEAN

NORTH AMERICA

John Cabot 1497 — EUROPE — A S I A

*Mississippi*

ATLANTIC OCEAN — PORTUGAL · Lisbon — BLACK SEA — CASPIAN SEA

Sagres — *Indus* — CHINA — 1543 — JAPAN

Columbus 1492 — Cairo · — Jerusalem · — *Ganges* — 1514 — PACIFIC OCEAN

Vespucci 1499–1500 — CARIBBEAN SEA — *Niger* — AFRICA — *Nile* — INDIA — · Macao

Equator — *Amazon* — Diaz 1487–88 — Da Gama 1497–99 — 1509 — · Malacca — Magellan 1519–22 — Equator

SOUTH AMERICA — *Zaire* — INDIAN OCEAN — THE MOLUCCAS

Magellan 1519–22 — *Zambezi*

AUSTRALIA

Strait of Magellan / Cape Horn — Cape of Good Hope — NEW ZEALAND

### Prince of navigators

The Portuguese were the first European seafarers to undertake exploration in a serious way. They owed much of their inspiration to Prince Henry (1394–1460), the son of King John I of Portugal and his English queen, Philippa. He set up a famous school of navigation at Sagres, which brought together the skills of navigators, geographers, mapmakers, astronomers, and boatbuilders. He also helped to organize a number of early Portuguese expeditions. By the time of his death, they had only reached the southern coasts of West Africa, but these were important first steps in the search for the route to the East.

He became known as Prince Henry the Navigator, although in fact he did not take part in any expeditions himself. Following his example, other schools of navigation were set up elsewhere in Europe, as depicted in this imaginative 1670 engraving. This was done despite the fact that the voyages Henry financed left him in debt when he died.

# SECTION 3: ASIA

**For thousands of years merchants and adventurers traveled along the trade routes that spanned Asia. But its mountains and areas of wilderness and desert ensured that its more remote corners remained unexplored until the 20th century.**

# FIRST CITIES

The origin of the word "civilization" is closely linked to the idea of citizens and cities. Towns and cities can exist only where people are well organized: they depend on farms to support them, on systems of trade, and on all kinds of professions to make them function properly. They also need efficient systems of law and government, and usually have well-developed religions.

Many of the world's first cities grew up in Asia, around 5,000 years ago, following the development of farming in about 9000 BC. Communities of farmers settled in the fertile lands around the major rivers, such as the Tigris and Euphrates in Mesopotamia, the Indus in southern Asia, and the Yellow (Hwang) River in China. As their farming became more efficient, their villages developed into towns, then cities. The first people to settle in Mesopotamia were the Sumerians who, after about 3500 BC, established centers of civilization which became

known as city-states. These encouraged the development of national identity among the people.

The civilizations of Mesopotamia, the Indus Valley, and China all developed along similar lines. They used the wheel for transportation; they developed networks of trade with many neighboring regions; each had its own form of writing. There was some communication between Mesopotamia and the civilizations of southern Asia. China, however, is walled in by the massive ridge of mountains that curls around the huge deserts of central Asia. It grew up more or less in isolation until trade routes opened up across the continent in the 2nd century BC.

The vast continent of Asia contains dramatic extremes of landscape and climate, including the Himalayas and Karakoram mountains, the burning deserts of Arabia, and the huge steppes of northern Asia, which lie frozen for much of the year. These have provided many of the greatest challenges in exploration.

**Left** Babylon was one of the world's first great cities and grew to become the capital of one of the major empires of Mesopotamia.

**Below** This clay tablet includes a very early map of the world with Babylon at the center.

**Civilization centered in towns and cities from c.3000 BC**

**Areas used by nomadic herders**

**Extent of trading area**

**Right** The ancient Chinese made bronze-casting into a fine art. This bronze wine vessel in the form of an owl dates from the 11th or 10th century BC.

**Below** The landscape of Asia has stood in the way of travelers, but has also provided protection from intruders. This fort is in the Hunza region of Pakistan.

**Above** Ancient civilizations centered upon the city-building cultures of Mesopotamia, ancient Egypt, the Indus Valley, and China. They were separated by landscapes of dramatic extremes, including the Himalayas and Karakoram mountains, and the burning deserts of Arabia. To the north lay treeless steppes, and the frozen wastelands of Siberia.

### Words and pictures

A system of writing called cuneiform developed in Mesopotamia in about 3000 BC, and Chinese writing began in about 1500 BC. In the beginning, words were represented by simple pictures of things. These "pictograms" gradually became more stylized with time.

### Birthplace of religions

Hinduism, Buddhism, Judaism, Christianity, and Islam all began in Asia, and are all closely connected to the development of civilization. Hinduism dates back 4,000 years and gave rise to some of the earliest great works of literature. The *Ramayana* tells the story (above) of how Prince Rama engages the help of the monkey army to rescue his wife, Sita. Hinduism is still the established faith in India, where it is practiced by millions of followers.

# EARLY CHINESE EXPLORERS

Chinese civilization began around 1700 BC, yet it took China over 1,000 years to make regular contact with the civilizations of western and southern Asia. In 138 BC Chang Ch'ien (who died about 112 BC) was sent to central Asia by Emperor Wu Ti (reigned 140–86 BC) to try to arrange treaties with peoples on the Chinese western borders against the invading Huns. He was away for 12 years, 10 of which he spent as a captive of the Huns. After he escaped, he tried to return to China via Tibet but was recaptured, although he eventually returned home. His mission was a failure, but he brought back news of trading opportunities with western Asia. As a result, new trade routes soon opened up, carrying such goods as spices, gems, and silk across the Gobi Desert and the high mountains of central Asia to the Middle East and Europe. There were several routes that became known generally as the "Silk Road."

Many of the early Chinese travelers to central and southern Asia were Buddhists in search of religious knowledge in and around northern India, the homeland of Buddhism. The most famous was Hsüan Tsang (AD 596–664). He traveled for 16 years across central Asia to Kashmir and India and along the River Ganges, and was welcomed home by the emperor. This was unusual, however, for travel beyond China's borders was not encouraged, and foreigners were kept out. For this reason, the advanced state of China's civilization remained virtually unknown to the West until Marco Polo's travels in the 13th century.

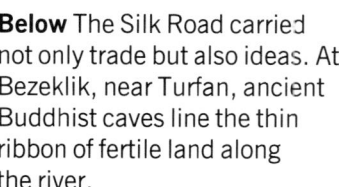

**Below** The Silk Road carried not only trade but also ideas. At Bezeklik, near Turfan, ancient Buddhist caves line the thin ribbon of fertile land along the river.

**Right** The Great Wall of China was begun in the 5th century BC and was more or less complete by 221 BC, although it was rebuilt and extended over a period of 2,000 years. Stretching for 2,150 miles (3,460 km), it was built to keep warring northern tribes out of China. For most Chinese it also marked the limit of civilization: beyond lay an unknown and barbaric world that they did not care to visit.

### The costliest cloth

Silk is manufactured by spinning the fibers from the cocoons of silkworms (right), the caterpillars of a moth which feed on mulberry trees. According to legend, it has been made since 2640 BC. The embroidered phoenix (left), found in the Altai mountains of central Asia, dates from the 4th century BC and is thought to be the oldest piece of silk in existence.

Silk cloth is very fine and has always been expensive. For thousands of years it was made only in China. In the 6th century AD, however, some silkworm eggs were smuggled out of China and taken to Constantinople (Istanbul). From these smuggled eggs, the development of the European medieval silk industry began.

**Left** War, trading opportunities, and Buddhism were the main inspiration behind the journeys of the great early Chinese travelers, journeys that took them into inland Asia and well beyond the self-imposed limits of Chinese civilization.

**Below** This bronze relief statue of Hsüan Tsang is from a temple dedicated to him in Taiwan. After 16 years of travel, Hsüan Tsang returned in triumph with a caravan bearing priceless religious texts and sacred relics.

➡ Hsüan Tsang   (AD 629-45)

➡ Chang Ch'ien (138-126 BC)

⇨ Northern silk route

⇨ Southern silk route

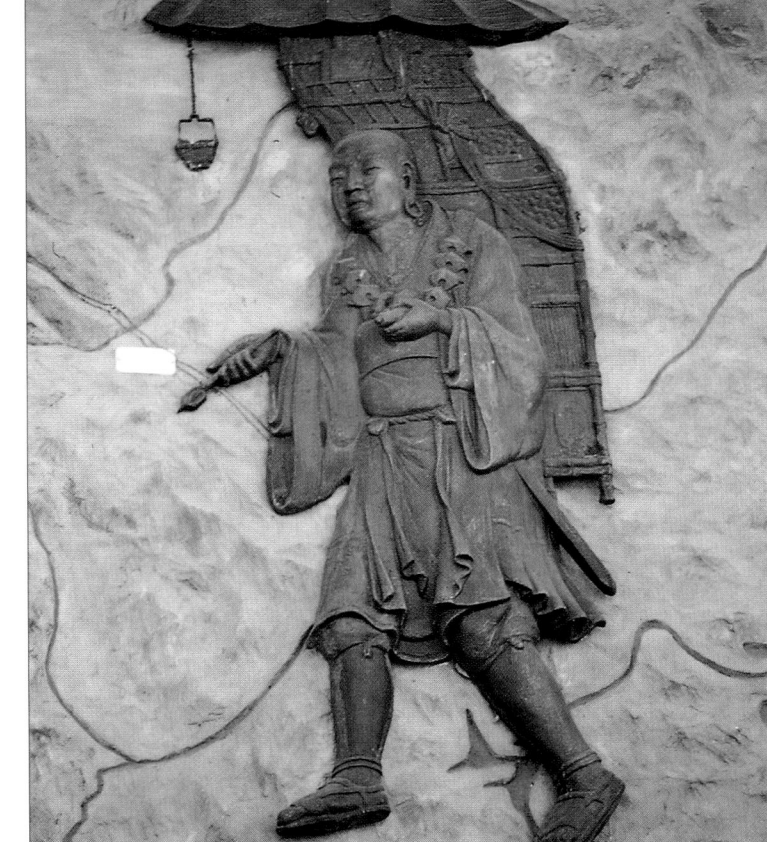

**Left** This gilt-bronze statue of a Bodhisattva (Buddha-to-be) was made in China in the 10th century AD, about 1,000 years after Buddhism had spread into China from India.

**Left** Although his forces were outnumbered three to one, Alexander defeated Darius III, the Persian king, decisively at the Battle of Issus in 333 BC. In a mosaic from the Roman city of Pompeii, Darius is seen in his chariot, and Alexander is on the left, mounted on his horse Bucephalus. Darius fled in defeat to Bactria.

# ALEXANDER THE GREAT

Alexander the Great (356–323 BC) was from Macedonia, a kingdom that came to dominate Greece during the reign of his father, King Philip II. As a boy, he was taught by the great philosopher Aristotle (384–322 BC).

When Alexander was 20 his father was murdered. He succeeded to the throne and began a series of conquests. In 334 BC he invaded the Persian Empire of Darius III (who ruled 336–330 BC); in 332 BC he entered Egypt and was crowned pharaoh; in 331 BC he finally defeated Darius and won control of the Persian Empire.

All along he took great trouble to collect information about the geography of the regions that fell to his conquests. For example, he sent an expedition led by Heracleides to establish whether or not the Caspian Sea was attached to the Black Sea, which several scholars believed to be the case.

After his victory over the Persians, he led his army on a great voyage of conquest and exploration, reaching the remote regions of Parthia, Bactria, and the Hindu Kush. By 326 BC he had reached the River Indus. By this time his armies were close to mutiny, so he turned back, taking the opportunity to send another expedition, under a general called Nearchus, to explore the Persian Gulf by sea.

All this was achieved in 13 years. During this time Alexander had traveled 20,000 miles (32,000 km) and founded 70 cities. Alexander was one of the greatest generals in history. When he died of fever in Babylon, he was just 32 years old.

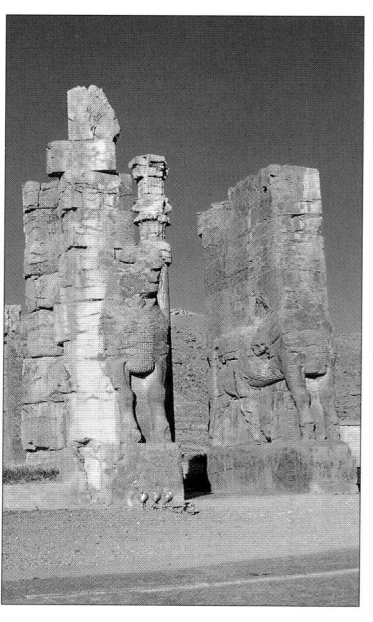

**Above** Persepolis was destroyed by Alexander in 330 BC. It had been built as the grand ceremonial capital of the Persian Empire by King Darius I (who ruled 522–486 BC), and only functioned fully once a year when ambassadors from all parts of the Empire came to deliver tribute to the king. The city was put to the torch by Alexander as an act of revenge for the earlier Persian burning of Athens.

**Measured by strides**

Alexander's armies were accompanied by teams of surveyors, geographers, mathematicians, and astronomers. Some of them went ahead to plan the advance of the armies; others mapped the conquered territories that extended from the River Indus to the eastern Mediterranean. The surveyors included men called *bematistae*, who measured distances by counting their strides. They wore sandals such as those pictured above. European maps made over 1,500 years later still used information about Asia acquired during Alexander's conquests.

BLACK SEA

CASPIAN SEA

MACEDONIA
GREECE

PHOENICIA

Amol

BACTRIA

PARTHIA

Babylon

BABYLONIA

Hindu Kush

Alexandria

PERSIA

Memphis

Persepolis

THE PERSIAN GULF

Indus

EGYPT

ARABIA

INDIA

⟹ Alexander the Great (334-323 BC)

➡ Nearchus (325-324 BC)

**Above** Alexander the Great swept through the eastern Mediterranean, destroying the Persian Empire. The thirst for exploration led him farther east, where he collected information that was still being used 1,500 years later.

**Below** No other European conqueror has succeeded as Alexander did in waging campaigns across the high mountains and deserts of central Asia. The landscape proved a tough and deadly challenge.

## The library of Alexandria

Alexandria, on the coast of northern Egypt, was founded by Alexander in 332 BC. About 30 years after his death a library was built there that was to become one of the great centers of learning of the ancient world. By the 2nd century BC it contained some 700,000 books (mainly in the form of papyrus scrolls). It was also famous for its cartography. Eratosthenes (the Greek who calculated the circumference of the Earth) was a librarian there, and Ptolemy was based at the library from AD 127–150 (see pages 10–11). It appears to have fallen from use by about the 7th century.

# THE RISE OF ISLAM

Ever since Roman times, the Middle East was a vital link between East and West. Trade came from China along the Silk Road (see pages 22–23) and across the Middle East to ports on the Mediterranean coast, or by sea from Southeast Asia and India to the Red Sea. Cities that controlled the trade routes soon became wealthy and powerful.

Muhammad (about AD 570–632), the prophet and founder of Islam, was born in Mecca, a trading city and an important religious center. His new religion spread with remarkable speed through conversion and conquest. Within a century of Muhammad's death, the Islamic Empire stretched from Spain in the west to Afghanistan in the east.

Islam quickly acquired a tradition for learning, and Muslim travelers set out across the Empire and beyond in a spirit of inquiry. Al-Masudi (who died AD 956) was one of the great Islamic travelers, and author of some 30 books. He traveled to Sri Lanka, China, and as far as the east coast of Africa.

The Islamic world also produced notable mapmakers and geographers, such as the north African Al-Idrisi (who died about 1165). He traveled all over the Islamic Empire before producing his famous map of the world, which was based largely on Greek sources.

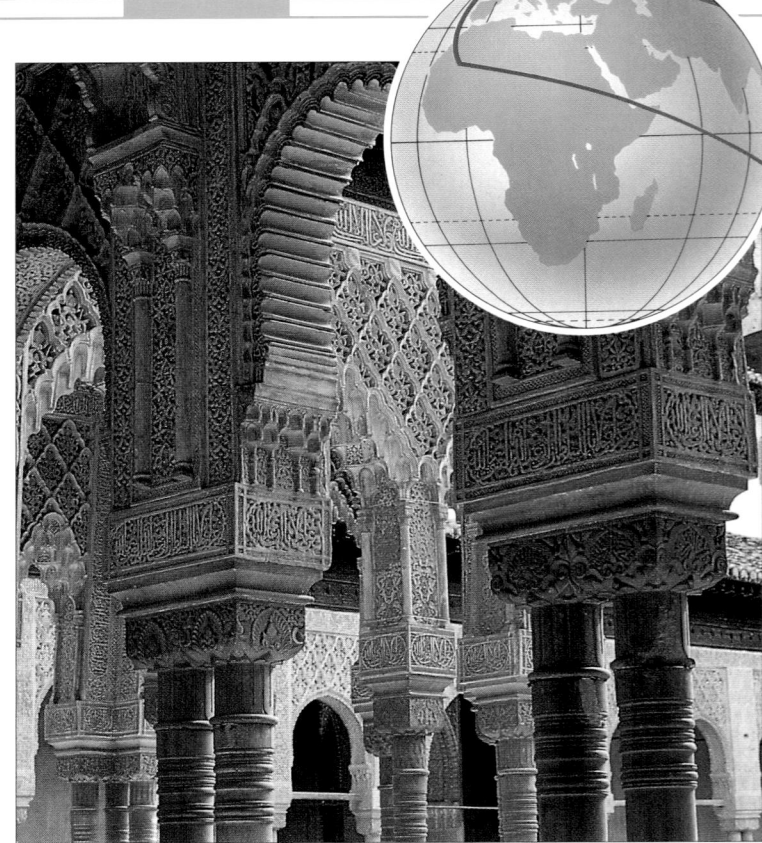

**Above** Muslims from northern Africa, known as the Moors, invaded Spain in AD 711, and parts of Spain remained under Muslim control until 1492. They built splendid mosques, and palaces such as this, the Alhambra in Granada.

**Right** The spread of Islam was swift and — with the sole major exception of Moorish Spain — lasting. By the 9th century it had taken over the southern Mediterranean and reached the borders of India.

**Below** The Kaaba, a cube-shaped stone building in the Great Mosque of Mecca, is the most sacred shrine of Islam. It contains the Black Stone which, according to tradition, is part of the first mosque, built by Abraham.

### Guided by the stars

The Arabs developed a number of important navigational instruments. They learned how to use the magnetic compass from the Chinese. They also perfected the astrolabe (above), a complex instrument for making calculations based on the stars. The instruments made them extremely skilled navigators.

## Guardians of learning

Despite their reputation for conquest, the rulers of the new Islamic Empire had great respect for learning. Baghdad, the capital of the Empire after AD 762, became a center for scholarship. While Europe descended into chaos, Islamic scholars led the world in medicine, astronomy, and mathematics, taking advantage of their connections with India, China, and the Greek scholars of Alexandria. They translated into Arabic the great works of Greek learning. These, as well as books by Arab writers, were later translated into Latin by European scholars during the Renaissance (see pages 18–19). This Latin translation (right) of an Arabic book, dating from the 13th century, shows a constellation represented in the form of an Arab-style ship.

Expansion of Islam under Muhammad

Expansion of Islam to 9th century

Direction of further expansion

## The battle for the Holy Lands

With the rise of Islam, the Christian world shrank. In earlier centuries the Christians had five main centers, or patriarchates. Jerusalem, Alexandria, and Antioch were lost to Islam in the 7th century, leaving just Constantinople in modern-day Turkey and Rome in Italy.

The European Christians eventually reacted by waging a series of wars, called Crusades, against Islam between the 11th and 13th centuries. Their purpose was to recapture their Holy Land, where Christ and the first Christians had lived and taught. But other important issues were also at stake, including territory and trade. The Christians only enjoyed temporary successes, such as the capture of Antioch in 1098 (left). In the early days of Islam, the Muslims had been tolerant of Christians, but the Crusades created a deep distrust which was to affect travel across the Middle East for centuries.

# THE MONGOLS AND MARCO POLO

During the early 13th century the Mongols united under their leader Genghis Khan (about 1167–1227). They then swept into China and across northern Asia. By 1241 these ruthless warriors had created an empire that stretched to the borders of Europe.

Several European ambassadors were dispatched to talk to the Mongol leaders. There was hope that they might be persuaded to join Christian Europe in its fight against the Islamic Empire.

In the 1260s two merchant brothers from Venice called Maffeo and Niccolò Polo went on a trading expedition across the Black Sea. Hostile Mongols prevented them from taking a direct route home, and the brothers ended up in China. By 1265 they had reached Beijing, then called Khanbalik, where they were treated well by the Mongol emperor of China, Kublai Khan. They returned home in 1269, but decided to make another trip to China two years later. This time they took Niccolò's 17-year-old son, Marco, with them. It was to be one of the great voyages of exploration of all time, lasting 24 years in all. Many of their tales of the wealth and splendor they had seen were not believed.

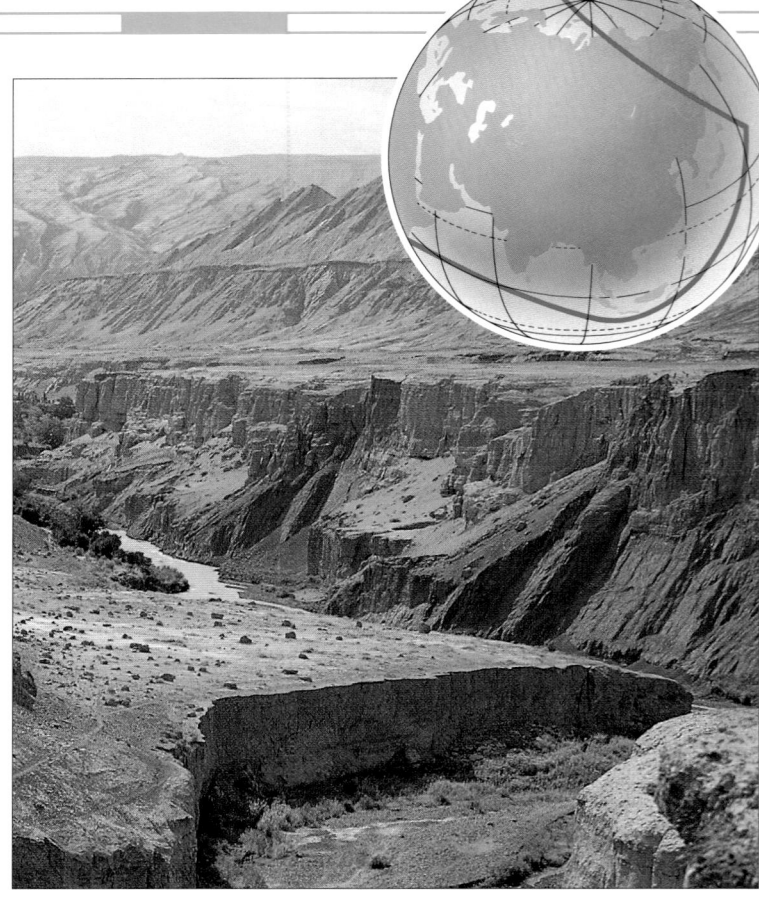

**Above** The landscape of central Asia was a formidable barrier to travelers attempting to reach the East. Mountainous wastelands, which are hot deserts in summer and bitterly cold in winter, gave little hint of the magnificent civilizations that lay beyond them.

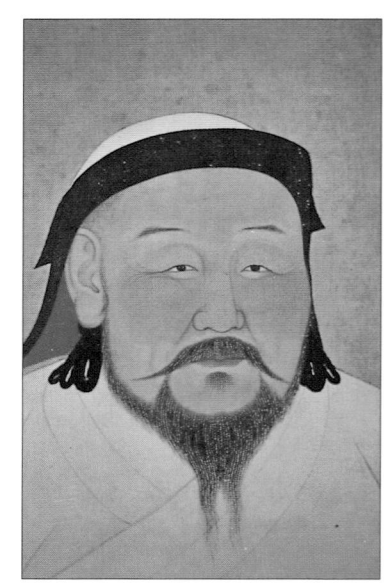

**Right** Marco Polo was treated with great favor by the emperor of China, Kublai Khan (about 1215–1294). He was the grandson of the great Genghis Khan.

## Marvels of China

Marco Polo came across many things in China that were quite unknown in Europe. The Chinese had invented gunpowder, which they used to make fireworks. They made printed books by using carved woodblocks. They even had paper money — an idea that seemed quite ridiculous to Europeans! Marco Polo also reported seeing mysterious "black stones, which they dig out and burn like firewood:" coal! When he wrote of such things, many people thought he was making them up.

## Prester John

In medieval times the Christians of Europe believed in the legend of Prester John, the ruler of a lost Christian kingdom somewhere in Asia. If such a kingdom existed, they thought, it could help the Crusaders to defeat the Muslims by attacking from the east. A similar rumor suggested that one of the Mongol leaders might be Christian. Prester John was not to be found in Asia, and so it was thought that his kingdom must be in East Africa.

SIBERIA

Novgorod

POLAND  RUSSIA

Urals

Venice

Danube  BLACK SEA

ARAL SEA

CASPIAN SEA

Samarkand

Kashi

Karakorum  Shangdu

MONGOLIA

Khanbalik (Beijing)

KOREA

JAPAN

Tabriz

MEDITERRANEAN SEA

Baghdad

Marco Polo (1271-75)

PERSIA

Indus

Himalayas

Delhi

Ganges

CHINA

Hwang

Yangtze

PACIFIC OCEAN

AFRICA  ARABIA

RED SEA

Nile

ARABIAN SEA

INDIA

BAY OF BENGAL

Greatest extent of Mongol Empire

Campaigns under Genghis Khan

Campaigns of his successors

Cochin  Marco Polo (1275-95)

SOUTH CHINA SEA

INDIAN OCEAN

BORNEO

**Above** The Mongol Empire spread over a vast area, the size of which can only really be appreciated by looking at the globe. Its violent, warring rulers presented a confusing picture to the Europeans, but as long as the trade routes were kept open, Europeans were happy to stay beyond its borders.

## Marco Polo

Marco Polo set off from Venice with his father and uncle in 1271 (right), and they traveled for three and a half years to reach Shangdu (or Xanadu), the summer capital of Kublai Khan. The Emperor was much impressed by Marco and decided to make him his ambassador. Over a period of 17 years Marco traveled to various parts of the Empire. The Polos' return journey took another three years. They reached Venice in 1295. Marco Polo died in 1324.

# THE QUEST FOR THE SPICE ISLANDS

Despite the reports of Marco Polo, it was not until the 15th century that the Portuguese began to make a determined effort to find the sources of the fabled riches of the East — in particular, spices.

In 1487 Pedro da Covilhã (see pages 46–47) reached India by crossing the Mediterranean and traveling down the Red Sea. What he found was a series of small independent states, many of which had become rich by trade with the Arab world.

Da Covilhã's reports made the Portuguese determined to find the sea route to the East. In 1498 Vasco da Gama became the first European explorer to reach India by sailing around the southern tip of Africa.

The Portuguese then began a series of aggressive naval expeditions. They established a fort on Sri Lanka in 1505 and captured Goa in 1510. But still they had not found the source of the spices, so they pushed on eastward. In 1511 an expedition of three ships sailed from Portuguese-controlled Malacca under the leadership of António de Abreu, and in the following year they reached the Banda Islands. This opened up the route to the Moluccas, then the only source of nutmeg and cloves in the world. The Portuguese had at last found the fabled Spice Islands.

Now they headed north to China and by the 1540s they had become the first Europeans to reach Japan.

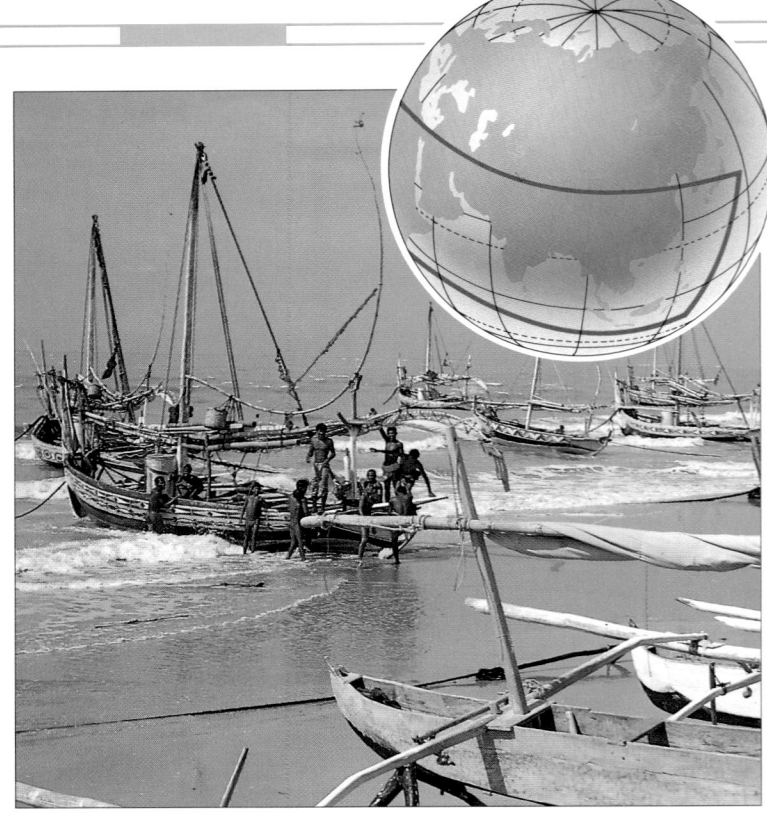

**Above** It was the lure of spices that brought the Europeans to Java and the other islands of Southeast Asia, but local traders and fishermen had sailed these seas for thousands of years before they arrived.

**Below** The Portuguese arrival in India opened the way for other European nations to begin trading with India, particularly the French, the British, and the Dutch (pictured here trading in Delhi).

### Passage to India

In 1497 the Portuguese naval captain Vasco da Gama (about 1460–1524) was commissioned by his king to see if it was possible to reach India by using the route around the southern tip of Africa, which Bartolomeu Dias had discovered in 1487 (see pages 46–47). Departing from Lisbon with four ships and 170 men, he sailed to Malindi on the east coast of Africa and engaged the services of some Arab pilots. They guided him to the port of Calicut, on the southwest coast of India, which he reached in May 1498. The Muslim traders here, however, were unimpressed by the goods that da Gama had brought; and they did not like the idea of Christian Europeans interfering with their trade. Nonetheless, da Gama was able to buy a few spices and other goods, proving that he had found the route to the East, and he returned to Portugal. Despite the fact that only 55 men out of the original 170 who had sailed with him survived, he was celebrated as a hero.

Da Gama made another trading expedition to India in 1502. In 1524 he returned to India as viceroy to govern the new Portuguese colonies, but unfortunately he died soon after his arrival in the country.

## Tightening their grip

Malacca (sometimes spelled Melaka) occupies a commanding position on the Strait of Malacca. Since a large proportion of Far Eastern trade passes through this channel, Malacca developed into one of the world's wealthiest trading ports.

In the early decades of the 16th century the Portuguese were determined to take control of the spice trade by force. Having captured Goa in India in 1510, Afonso de Albuquerque headed eastward to Malacca, which he captured in 1511.

Soon the Portuguese had established their own colony in Malacca, and by the 1520s they had taken over the production of cloves and nutmeg (left) in the "Spice Islands."

**Left** Spices were the real goal of the European explorers in the 15th and 16th centuries; where the spices lay, so did the riches of the Orient — as far as they knew. Like a treasure hunt, the search led them stage by stage from Africa to India and eventually to the Spice Islands in Southeast Asia.

PERSIA
THE GULF
Hormuz
Indus
Delhi
Ganges
CHINA
RED SEA
ARABIA
ARABIAN SEA
INDIA
BURMA
Mekong
INDOCHINA
Bombay
BAY OF BENGAL
SIAM
SOUTH CHINA SEA
PACIFIC OCEAN
PHILIPPINE ISLANDS
Goa
Calicut
AFRICA
SRI LANKA
MALAYA
Malacca
Strait of Malacca
Mogadishu
SUMATRA
BORNEO
MOLUCCAS
CELEBES
CERAM
NEW GUINEA
Malindi
INDIAN OCEAN
JAVA
TIMOR
ARAFURA SEA
MADAGASCAR

➡ Da Covilhã (1487-90)

➡ Da Gama (1498-99)

➡ Albuquerque (1507-11)

➡ Abreu (1511)

## Precious spices

Spices originally grew only in southern Asia and Southeast Asia. Cinnamon came from Sri Lanka; nutmeg and cloves came from the Moluccas; pepper came from various islands of Southeast Asia; and ginger came mainly from China.

Spices are excellent trade goods. They are easy to handle and look after, and large quantities can be broken up into smaller and smaller portions for sale. In Europe they were used to preserve meat over winter and to flavor food, as well as to make medicines and perfumes. But before the Europeans had direct access to the places where spices were grown, they were very expensive. Once the European nations had control of the trade, prices began to drop.

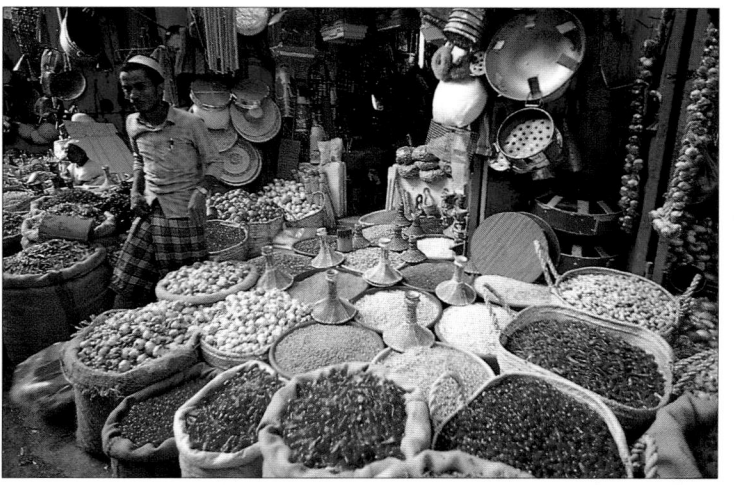

31

# REMOTE ASIAN LANDS

Much of central Asia and Japan remained beyond the reach of all but a few travelers for many centuries.

The Chinese were always suspicious of foreigners. The Ming Dynasty (1368–1644) turned its back on the outside world — apart from the brief spell under Emperor Ch'eng Tsu in the early 15th century (see pages 44–45).

The Portuguese had reached Japan in the 1540s, closely followed by missionaries, including St. Francis Xavier. The Christian population of Japan grew to about 300,000 before a new *shogun* (feudal lord) called Tokugawa Ieyasu began to persecute them in about 1615. Foreigners were expelled and Japanese citizens were expressly forbidden to travel abroad.

In central Asia and Tibet both the mountainous landscape and the hostility of governments stood in the way of exploration. Rare exceptions include some Christian missionaries who reached Tibet in 1611, and a Briton called Thomas Manning who reached Lhasa in 1811.

The French missionaries Abbé Huc and Joseph Gabet traveled through China under the most gruelling conditions to reach Tibet in 1846, only to be expelled after six weeks. Their book, *Travels in Tartary, Tibet and China,* excited the imagination of other explorers. But because of its inaccessibility, Tibet remained within the sights of only the most determined and persistent travelers until well into the 20th century.

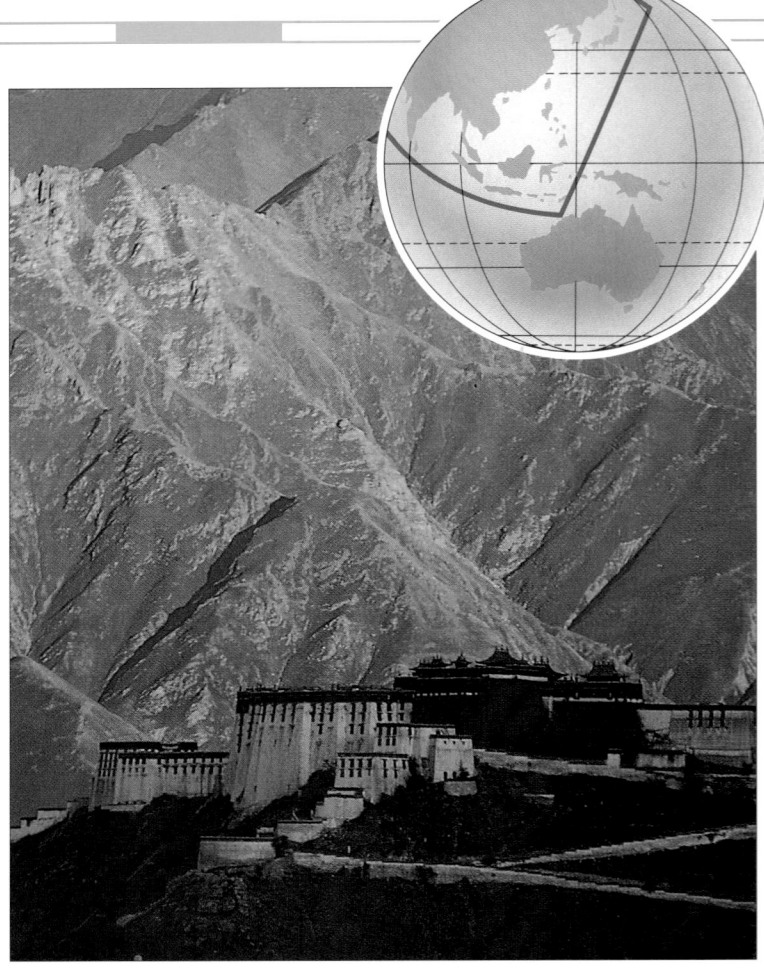

**Above** The Potala Palace looms over Lhasa, the capital of Tibet, perched on a massive rock. This was the home of the Dalai Lama, or ruler of Tibet, until 1959.

**Below** The delicate architecture of this building in Kyoto, the capital of Japan until 1868, is an example of the unique qualities of Japanese culture.

## "Apostle of the Indies"

St. Francis Xavier (1506–1552) was a Spanish missionary who was one of the founders of the Roman Catholic Jesuit movement. He traveled to southern Asia, making numerous converts in Goa, Sri Lanka, and the Moluccas, before reaching Japan in 1549.

## Prayers on the wind

Travelers in the Himalayas have always been fascinated by the traditions of Tibetan Buddhism. Since their invasion of Tibet in 1950, the Chinese have destroyed many of the great monasteries there. But Buddhism lives on. Prayer flags and prayer wheels (below) are used in a constant round of prayers.

**Above** Travelers in the Himalayas face unusual challenges, from the weather as well as the mountainous landscape. Even today, in some areas there are no roads, and traders, travelers, pilgrims, and administrators have to use a network of ancient paths to travel between remote villages. Rivers may be spanned by bridges made of bamboo or rope that would deter all but the most dauntless traveler.

## Parisian lady in Lhasa

In the 19th century the British controlled most of India, but they were always concerned about India's northern borders with the rest of Asia. In 1903 Sir Francis Younghusband, himself a great traveler of the region, arranged a treaty with the Tibetans to keep all non-British people out.

Nonetheless, a French explorer called Alexandra David-Néel (1868–1969) wanted to visit Tibet, and being turned back by the British in 1912 only made her more determined. Guided by a Buddhist monk called Aphur Yongden, she spent 12 years traveling in Sikkim, Tibet, and China, and studying Buddhism and the Tibetan language. Disguised as a poor Tibetan pilgrim, she eventually succeeded in reaching Lhasa in 1924. She was the first Western woman to have achieved this. Her account of the journey, *Travels of a Parisian Lady in Lhasa*, was published in 1928.

**Above** From around 1540 to 1639 Japan was open to foreigners, notably European missionaries. But after this it remained shut off from the rest of the world. Explorers were prevented from reaching the remote regions of the Himalayas, especially Tibet, by the awesome landscape, as well as by deliberate policy to keep them out.

→ Xavier and other Jesuits (1540-1622)

→ Abbé Huc (1844-46)

→ Alexandra David-Néel (1921-24)

# THE NORTHEAST PASSAGE

By the 1570s the Portuguese and the Spanish were in control of the routes to the Far East across the southern oceans. Other European nations wanted to find sea routes either westward around the north of America (a route they called the Northwest Passage), or eastward around the north of Russia (which they referred to as the Northeast Passage).

The first explorer to make a serious attempt to find the Northeast Passage was the Dutchman Willem Barents, who led three expeditions in the 1590s and reached Novaya Zemlya before being defeated by ice.

By the 1720s the Russians still did not know if their country was joined to North America. The Danish explorer Vitus Bering (about 1680–1741) was commissioned to investigate. In 1728 he sailed between Russia and Alaska through the strait now named after him, but fog prevented him from being sure that this stretch of water separated Russia from North America.

The mapping of the northern seas over the next century proved that a Northeast Passage did exist. But the first man to sail along it was the Swedish Finn Baron Adolf Nordenkiöld in 1878–1879. Powerful ice-breaking ships were used to forge a route in 1910, and since the 1930s the passage has been used regularly by Russian ships.

**Below** The land to the north of Russia lies well inside the Arctic Circle and is ice-bound for 10 months every year.

**Above** Barents's expedition spent the winter of 1596–1597 in a house built from the timbers of their ship. In June 1597 they set out for the south in open boats. Barents died, but 12 men survived.

**Left** In 1596 Barents reached Spitzbergen and crossed the sea now named after him to northern Novaya Zemlya. Here his ship was trapped and crushed by ice as the Arctic winter set in.

## Map

NORTH PACIFIC OCEAN

BERING ISLANDS

ALEUTIAN ISLANDS

BERING SEA

Kamchatka Peninsula

Bering Strait

ALASKA

SIBERIA

BEAUFORT SEA

A S I A

LAPTEV SEA

ARCTIC OCEAN

North Pole

KARA SEA

NOVAYA ZEMLYA

SPITZBERGEN

BARENTS SEA

GREENLAND

E U R O P E

NORWAY

ICELAND

Stockholm

BALTIC SEA

**Above** Explorers in search of the Northeast Passage had to cut a path through the Arctic Circle, which was locked in ice for most of the year. This view of the world from over the North Pole demonstrates vividly the difficulty of the task.

→ Barents (1594-95)
⇢ Barents (1596-97)
→ Bering (1728)
➡ Bering (1741)
⇨ Nordenkiöld (1878-79)

### Vitus Bering

Vitus Bering oversaw the Great Northern Expedition of 1733-1743, which mapped much of the coast of Siberia and Alaska. He himself mapped eastern Siberia and then the southern parts of Alaska with the intention of claiming Alaska for Russia. (Alaska was Russian until 1867 when it was sold to the United States.) However, Bering died of scurvy on the return journey in 1741.

The discovery of the Bering Strait suggested that this could be the possible exit for the Northeast Passage. It was also the exit for the Northwest Passage, but it was 100 years before this was proved by a British party led by Commander Robert McLure, which sailed northward through the Bering Strait in 1850. After being rescued from disaster, the expedition was taken eastward, reaching Baffin Bay in eastern Canada in 1854.

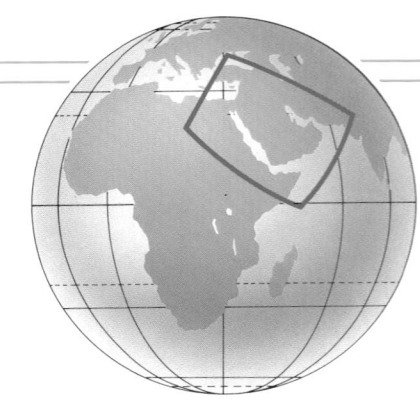

# TRAVELS IN ARABIA

Since the Crusades during the Middle Ages, the Muslims of the Arab world looked upon outsiders from Christian Europe with great distrust. Christian travelers were liable to be imprisoned, beaten or killed — especially if they tried to enter the holy cities of Islam such as Mecca and Medina. Nonetheless, some brave travelers did succeed in reaching these places, including the Portuguese Pedro da Covilhã in 1492 (see pages 30–31).

During the early 19th century the European nations began to create various trading stations around the coasts of the Arabian peninsula, but the interior remained a blank on the map. The fact that so little was known about this region, or the people who lived there, began to excite great curiosity.

Arabia became an explorer's challenge. There were few rewards here in terms of trade or conquest: travelers in this region were usually scholars in daring pursuit of knowledge, such as Johann Burckhardt or Charles Doughty; or scholar-adventurers in search of glory, such as Richard Burton and Harry St. John Philby. To survive in this hostile environment, they usually had to study Arabic and Islam, and disguise themselves as Arab travelers. Even so they had to pay enormous attention to detail in all aspects of their speech and dress. The slightest mistake could mean detection and possible death.

The exploration of Arabia by Europeans took well over a century. The Empty Quarter, the most hostile part of the Arabian peninsula, remained unexplored until the 1930s.

### A British adventurer

Richard Burton (1821–1890) was one of the outstanding explorers of the Victorian age. He had a wildly adventurous and unpredictable nature, but he was highly capable and had an exceptional gift for learning foreign languages. In 1853, while serving as an officer in the British Indian Army, he was given permission to travel in Arabia. Disguised as a Muslim doctor, he joined the pilgrimage to the sacred Muslim shrines of Mecca and Medina. Four years later he traveled to East Africa with Speke in search of the source of the Nile (see pages 50–51).

### Desert dwellers

The Bedouin are nomadic people who have traditionally inhabited desert regions of the Middle East. (The word in Arabic means "desert dwellers.") They make their livelihood from their sheep and camels, and move their tents from place to place in search of pasture. They know exactly where water can be found, and can survive in the most difficult conditions where those who do not have their knowledge would soon die.

Charles Doughty (1843–1926) lived and traveled with the Bedouin for eight months in 1876. He refused to disguise the fact that he was a Christian, and so was treated with suspicion. But he learned a great deal about the hardships of their lives, as well as their traditions of kindness and hospitality.

Doughty was in the Middle East for two years, and took another 10 years to write up his notes. His book, *Travels in Arabia Deserta*, is one of the classics of travel writing.

### A lost world carved in stone

Johann Burckhardt (1784–1817) was a Swiss scholar working in England, who was chosen by the African Association (see pages 48–49) to make an expedition across the Sahara Desert. He went to Syria in 1809 to learn Arabic and study Islam, then set off on an overland trip to Cairo. It was on this journey that he came across the ruins of the lost city of Petra (right), carved out of pink sandstone and hidden in a remote valley. This was once the capital of the Nabataeans, founded in the 4th century BC and an early center for Christianity.

After reaching Cairo, he traveled south along the Nile, where he discovered the now famous temple of Abu Simbel. Then, disguised as an Egyptian Arab, he crossed the Red Sea to Mecca. He returned to Cairo in 1815, and died there in 1817.

**Below** European travelers had reached parts of the Arabian peninsula as early as the 15th century, and several had managed to infiltrate Mecca, the most sacred city of Islam. But the interior remained one of the last great challenges of Asian exploration.

**Right** During the First World War, T.E. Lawrence fought alongside the Arabs in their struggle against the Turks. His knowledge of the Arabs and their way of life became so acute that he became known as Lawrence of Arabia.

### The Queen of Sheba

According to legend, the Queen of Sheba visited King Solomon in the 10th century BC. The Old Testament says she came to seek the King's wisdom, but the most likely reason was to establish trade links. This temple, at Marib in Yemen, is said to commemorate her visit.

- Burckhardt (1812)
- Burckhardt (1813-15)
- Burton (1853-54)
- Doughty (1875)
- Doughty (1876-78)
- Philby (1932)

# SECTION 4: AFRICA

**Africa has produced the earliest traces of human life, dating back 3 or 4 million years ago. The ancient Egyptians developed one of the first great civilizations. Yet Africa remained a mystery to the outside world.**

## THE FIRST HUMANS

Africa could claim to be the birthplace of humankind. Early forms of human beings originated in Africa about 2 million years ago, then migrated to populate the rest of the world.

Much more recently, about 6,000 years ago, the fertile valley of the River Nile provided the right conditions for the civilization of ancient Egypt to take root. By 2500 BC the first pyramids had been completed — some of the world's great marvels of engineering and the only one of the seven wonders of the ancient world still standing.

Yet African civilization was to remain different from that of the Mediterranean and Asia. South of the Sahara, traditions of herding, farming, and trading seldom led to ambitious town-building. Great Zimbabwe is a rare exception.

Meanwhile Arab, European, even Chinese traders found what they wanted along the coasts, and for centuries the heartlands of Africa remained virtually undisturbed by outsiders from other continents.

### First of the line

The modern form of human beings (*Homo sapiens*) has only been in existence for 100,000 years. Since Darwin proposed that humans descended from apelike ancestors (see pages 64–65), researchers have hoped to find the remains of earlier human forms. Traces of various hominids, the earliest humanlike forms, such as this skull, have been found in East Africa. *Australopithecus afarensis* dates back about 4 million years. But *Homo habilis*, of 2 million years ago, is more likely to be the ancestor of modern human beings. Traces of *Homo habilis* have been found in the Olduvai Gorge in the Rift Valley of East Africa. *Homo habilis* was the first creature to use rough-cut flints for tools.

**Above** Great Zimbabwe was a major trading center that flourished during the African Iron Age, between AD 1000 and 1450. The massive stone walls give some idea of the town. It was not until the 18th century that Europeans began to appreciate the potential that Africa held. By the mid-19th century the scramble for territory in Africa was at its height. Zimbabwe became part of the British Empire, as Southern Rhodesia. When it achieved independence, it reverted to its original name.

**Left** The Sahara has always provided a barrier to travel, although trading caravans have crossed the desert for centuries. As a result, the people and cultures of North Africa have always remained separate from those to the south of the desert.

**Below** Archaeological finds in East Africa suggest that this was a center for early forms of the human species. Human development generally followed a southward movement in Africa. The practice of cattle farming, then the use of iron, gradually spread throughout the continent from the Mediterranean coasts.

**Above** Some of Africa's finest works of art came from the kingdom of Benin, which flourished from the 13th to the 17th century.

**Below** The mud houses of the Dogon people of Mali demonstrate how traditional African life has survived in some of the inland parts of Africa.

MEDITERRANEAN SEA

Atlas Mountains

Thebes

RED SEA

A F R I C A

4500 BC

Nile

ARABIA

Sahara
Desert

3000 BC

Kingdom of
Meroe
900 BC-AD 400

Early human migration

2000 BC

Early human migration

Senegal

MALI

1500 BC

Ethiopian
Highlands

BENIN

Niger

ATLANTIC
OCEAN

500 BC

Zaire

Lake Victoria

Great Rift Valley

Olduvai Gorge

INDIAN
OCEAN

Limits of cattle domestication

Spread of iron

AD 500

Zambezi

AD 1000

Great Zimbabwe

MADAGASCAR

Limpopo

Kalahari
Desert

Orange

# ANCIENT EGYPT

The civilization of ancient Egypt developed over 5,000 years ago. It was centered on the fertile and navigable stretches of the River Nile to the north of the First Cataract (a point on the river where waterfalls occur). This is part of the "Fertile Crescent," which also saw the birth of civilizations in Mesopotamia, in the land between the Tigris and Euphrates rivers.

Ancient Egypt developed links with the other kingdoms and peoples of the Middle East, but expeditions to the rest of Africa lying to the south seem to have been few and far between. The rare exceptions were recorded in elaborate inscriptions. A famous example is a major expedition carried out under the orders of Queen Hatshepsut in 1492 BC to the "Land of Punt," which is believed to be somewhere in the region of modern Somalia.

At various times Phoenicia came within the Empire of Egypt. In about 600 BC, Pharaoh Necho II commissioned a Phoenician fleet to find a route from the Red Sea to the Mediterranean. They appear to have achieved this by sailing around the Cape of Good Hope. They reported seeing the sun on their right as they traveled from east to west around the southern tip of Africa — but because people living in the northern hemisphere would have had no experience of this, many disbelieved their story.

The Phoenicians were the great seamen of their time, and had traveled beyond the Strait of Gibraltar to Madeira and the Canary Islands by the 7th century BC, where they traded in dye. General Hanno, from Carthage, led a huge fleet in this direction in 470 BC and continued his journey down much of the west coast of Africa.

The story of the expedition to Punt is told in a series of inscriptions (left) on the walls of Deir el-Bahri (above), the vast temple to the west of Thebes built by the powerful Queen Hatshepsut (who reigned 1501–1479 BC). The inscriptions seen here show living myrrh trees arriving in Thebes — presumably after being carried in their pots from the Red Sea to the River Nile.

## The voyage to Punt

Like many journeys of exploration, the expedition to the Land of Punt in 1492 BC was primarily concerned with trade. Records of the expedition speak glowingly of the vast quantities of goods brought back by the expedition ships, pictured fully laden on the walls of Deir el-Bahri (right). These included incense, ebony, ivory, gold and silver, and live monkeys.

## The world's first explorer?

In about 2300 BC an official called Harkhuf was sent on expeditions to Yam, in Nubia. By traveling beyond the First Cataract of the River Nile, he crossed the farthest limit of the known world of the ancient Egyptians. A record of his journeys was found in inscriptions on his tomb at Elephantine Island (left), on the Nile.

## Sacred cargoes

The ancient Egyptians preserved the bodies of their dead by embalming them with various salts, resins, oils, and ointments — a process overseen by the jackal-headed god Anubis. Many of the precious substances they used in the process, such as myrrh and frankincense, had to be imported from abroad.

**Nehsi's expedition for Queen Hatshepsut (1492 BC)**

**Circumnavigation of Africa under Pharaoh Necho (600 BC)**

**Hanno (470 BC)**

**Left** Given the time span of a thousand years, the progress of Egyptian exploration was slow, and focused primarily on the coasts of Africa and the pursuit of trade. Even Pharaoh Necho's daring expedition around Africa was inspired by his wish to find a trade route that could link the Red Sea to the Nile Delta.

The expedition would have gone overland from Thebes to join ocean-going ships on the Red Sea, which then sailed about 1,250 miles (2,000 km) down the Red Sea to Punt. The astonished reaction of the people of Punt, recorded in the inscriptions at Deir el-Bahri, indicates that this was genuinely a journey of exploration, not a regular trading mission.

# ARAB TRAVELERS IN AFRICA

Within 70 years of the death of the Prophet Muhammad (see pages 26–27), Islam had spread across the length of North Africa bringing the Arab influence to Egypt, Libya, Tunisia, Algeria, and Morocco.

The Arabs were quick to exploit the trading routes from North Africa to West Africa, traveling across the Sahara from oasis to oasis in caravans of camels. With trade came Islam. These caravan routes were soon used by Muslim pilgrims on their way to and from Mecca, a journey that could take five or more years. One pilgrim from North Africa was Ibn Battuta (1304–1377), who was celebrated as the most widely traveled man of his day.

By the 13th century West Africa had become the world's most important source of gold. When several travelers reported on the fabulous wealth of Timbuktu, it became legendary for European adventurers. But they did not reach Timbuktu for 300 years.

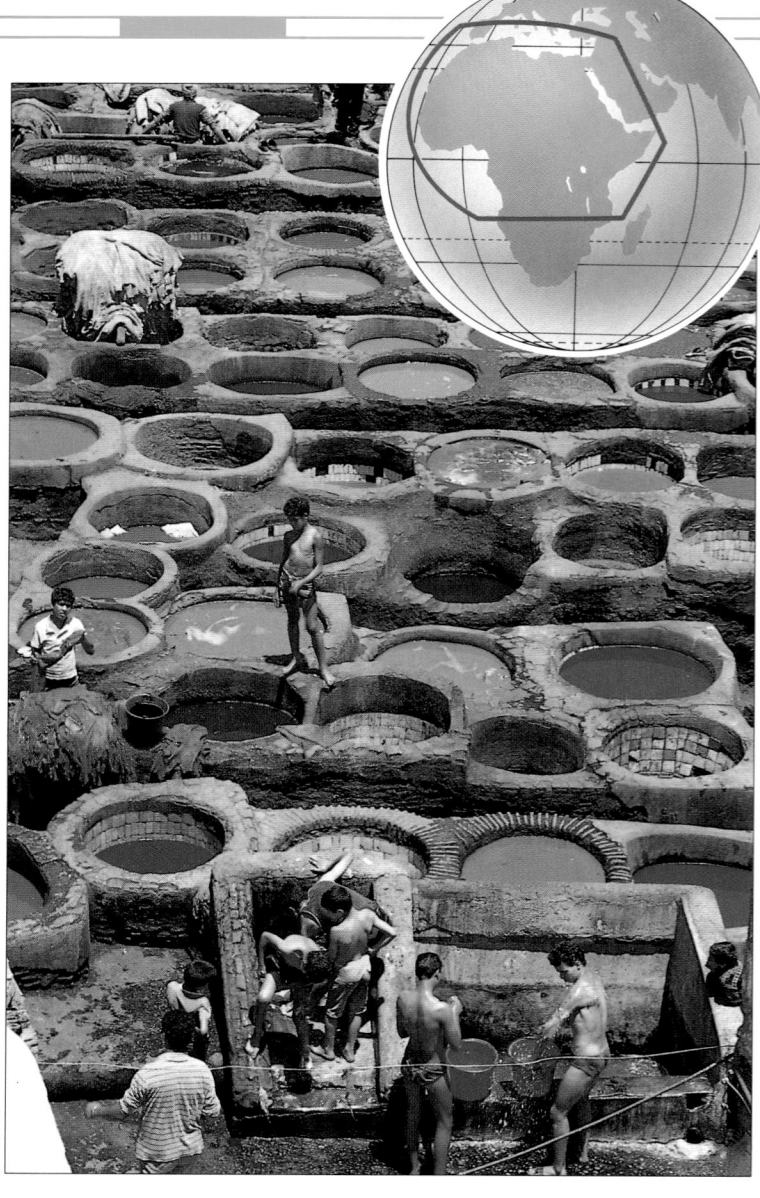

**Above** Ibn Battuta wrote his accounts of his journeys in Fez, Morocco, where he settled at the end of his travels after a journey to West Africa. A major trading center, Fez is famous for its dye-works, where wool is still dyed in traditional open-air vats. It is also a center of Islamic learning, with one of the world's oldest universities, founded in AD 850.

**Below** The Arabs were skilled traders, and for centuries controlled all trade between Asia and Europe, much of which came up the Red Sea and then overland to Alexandria. In West Africa they exchanged salt and various luxury goods for gold and slaves. The routes across the Sahara were difficult and dangerous, but the rewards were great. Merchants such as these could make great fortunes on one trip alone.

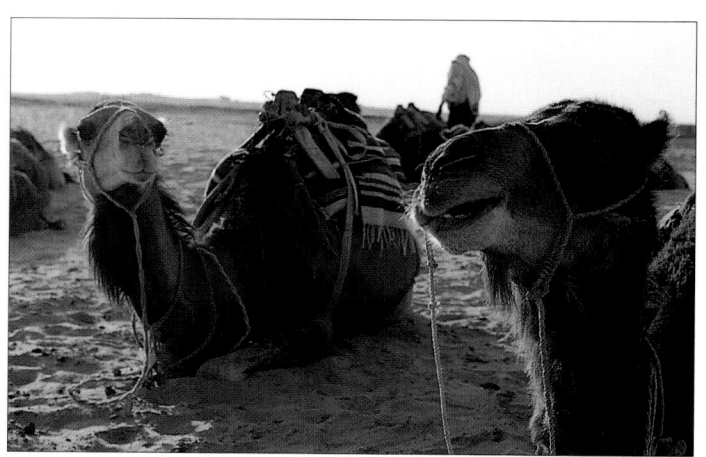

### Ships of the desert

Ibn Battuta (1304–1377) was born in Tangier, Morocco. In 1325 he decided to make the pilgrimage to Mecca — the start of some 30 years of travel. His route took him to Jerusalem and Damascus, where he became a teacher of Islam. After studying law in Mecca, he began a series of journeys that took him to the most far-flung places of the world that had been reached by Islam. He sailed down the Red Sea to East Africa, then went north to the Black Sea and on to India and China. He joined a trading caravan across the western Sahara to West Africa, traveling with "ships of the desert" — camels. After his final return to Morocco in 1354 he had traveled 75,000 miles (120,000 km).

## Islam in Africa

As in India and Southeast Asia, Islam spread to East and West Africa mainly through trade, not conquest. Islam also spread down the River Nile to Sudan, and to the countries to the south of the Sahara. It reached West Africa by the caravan routes across the Sahara.

Islam was adopted by the Mali Empire after AD 1000. The wealth of these West African Muslims became famous: in 1324 King Mansa Musa took so much gold with him on his pilgrimage to Mecca that he unbalanced the economies of countries on his route.

Islam is still a strong force in Africa today, as witnessed by the men (right) attending prayers at a mosque in Burkina.

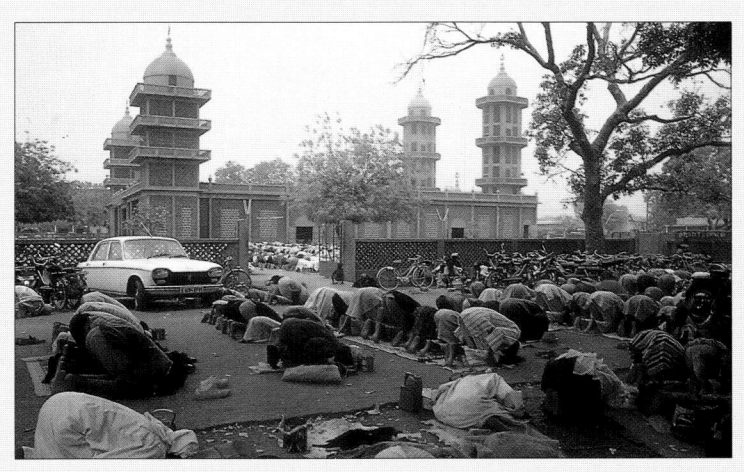

➡ Principal trade routes

➡ Secondary trade routes

Ibn Battuta's voyages:

➡ 1325-27

➡ 1327-30

➡ 1330-49

➡ 1349-54

**Left** Timbuktu was the capital of the Mali Empire in the 14th century and grew rich on trade in salt and gold. After being sacked by the Moroccans in 1593, however, it went into decline, by which time it had acquired legendary status among Europeans.

**Above** The Arabs exploited established trade links across the Sahara to the nations of West Africa. These routes were used by explorers in the 14th century, and European explorers 500 years later. Ibn Battuta also took advantage of the sea routes used by Arab traders.

# ACROSS THE INDIAN OCEAN

As early as the 9th century, East Africa had trading connections that stretched to the Arab world, India, to Southeast Asia, and even China. Arab merchants had settled in the ports, such as Zanzibar, where they traded in ivory, rhinoceros horn, gold, and slaves, receiving in return spices, silks, and Chinese porcelain, some of which they traded with Europeans.

Chinese merchants were known to have visited the Middle East by sea as early as AD 360, and had certainly reached Zanzibar and Madagascar by the 1180s. However, these were exceptions. The Chinese were only able to explore beyond their own borders during certain periods of their history.

One of these periods occurred under Emperor Ch'eng Tsu in the early Ming Dynasty (1368–1644). He put a Muslim courtier, Admiral Cheng Ho, or Zheng Ho (1371–1435), in charge of a massive fleet, to undertake a series of seven voyages of exploration from 1405 to 1433. They had reached Africa by 1415. They may even have rounded the Cape of Good Hope some 70 years before the first Europeans did so.

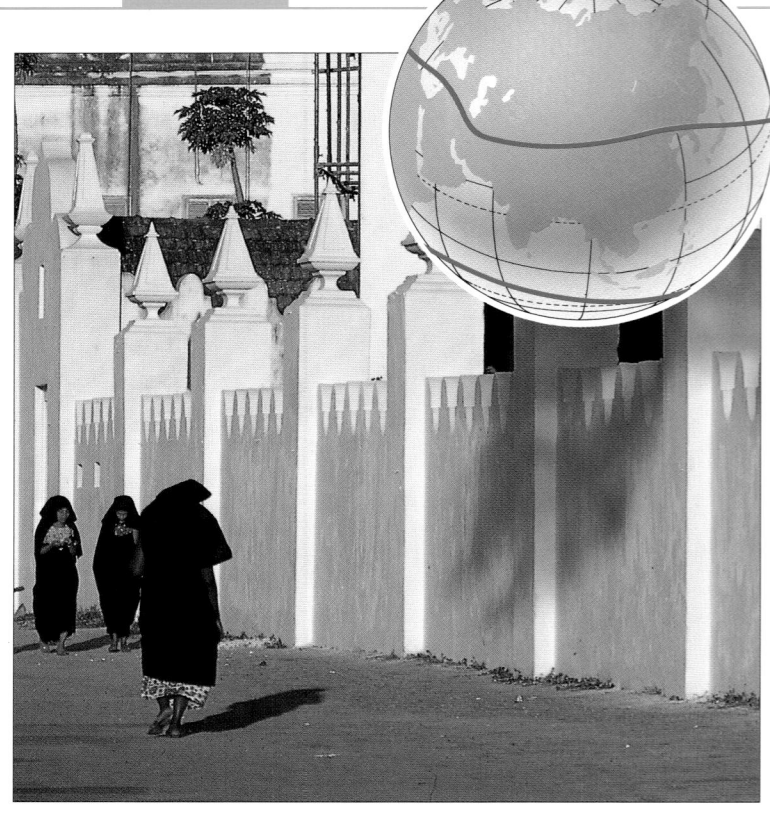

**Above** Zanzibar was one of several wealthy trading ports on the East African coast where Arab traders settled, bringing Islam with them. Arabs were the chief slave traders until the 19th century.

**Below** This picture of a Chinese man leading a zebra dates from 1430. A number of African animals reached China during the period of Cheng Ho's voyages, usually as gifts to the emperor.

### Precious china

By the 10th century the Chinese had mastered the technique of producing a kind of pottery called porcelain. It was made from a mixture of clays then found only in China, and was finer than any other pottery in the world. As a result it became highly prized, and was laboriously carried across Asia on the Silk Road (see pages 22–23) to Europe, and across the Indian Ocean to Africa. Pieces of porcelain have been found in the old Arab trading port of Kilwa on the East African coast.

After the Dutch East India Company came to dominate the trade in the 17th century, tons of Chinese porcelain were shipped all over the world. Europe started to produce its own porcelain in the 18th century.

RED SEA · Jeddah · ARABIA · Dhofar · La'sa · Aden · AFRICA · Mogadishu · Malindi · ZANZIBAR · Kilwa · Nile · PERSIA · THE GULF · Hormuz · Indus · Himalayas · Ganges · Gaur · INDIA · ARABIAN SEA · Calicut · SRI LANKA · MALDIVE ISLANDS · BAY OF BENGAL · INDIAN OCEAN · CHINA · Yangtze · Mekong · Nanking · PACIFIC OCEAN · CAMBODIA · MALAY PENINSULA · SOUTH CHINA SEA · PHILIPPINE ISLANDS · SUMATRA · BORNEO · Semarang · JAVA

Cheng Ho's journeys

➡ outward (1431-33)

➡ return (1433)

➡ additional voyages

**Above** Cheng Ho's epic journeys from 1405 to 1433 pieced together the numerous trading links that spanned the southern oceans.

**Below** Cheng Ho's fleet consisted mainly of junks. Some of these were five times the size of the Portuguese caravels.

## Cheng Ho

Cheng Ho's fleet was probably the largest that ever sailed in the name of exploration. He was in command of 27,000 men and 317 ships, and his expeditions consisted of as many as 63 ships sailing together. His seven voyages lasted about two years each. The fleet traveled through much of Southeast Asia, visiting ports such as Semarang (above), in Java, and perhaps even sailing to the north coast of Australia. Other expeditions went to India, the Persian Gulf, and the east coast of Africa.

Their purpose was to trade, to collect taxes from Chinese colonies, and to gather information.

After Emperor Ch'eng Tsu died, Cheng Ho fell from favor. He was allowed to make one more voyage ending in 1433 before China once more turned its back on the outside world. One hundred years later the Europeans had explored much of the world that Cheng Ho had reached. If Cheng Ho's achievements had been maintained, the history of exploration might have been different.

# EARLY EUROPEAN EXPLORERS

During the first decades of the 15th century, the Portuguese began a series of voyages down the west coast of Africa in their search for a sea route to the Far East. In 1434 Gil Eannes became the first navigator to dare to sail south of Cape Bojador. Fifty years later, in 1487, Bartolomeu Dias rounded the Cape of Good Hope at the tip of southern Africa.

That same year, Pedro da Covilhã and Afonso da Paiva crossed the Mediterranean and traveled down the Red Sea. Da Paiva went in search of Prester John in East Africa (see pages 28–29), but disappeared. Da Covilhã reached India, and later went to live in Abyssinia (Ethiopia). Meanwhile, in 1497 Vasco da Gama sailed up the east coast of Africa and finally found the sea route to India (see pages 30–31) that European adventurers had been hoping to discover for many years.

On the way to the East, the Portuguese discovered the rich trading possibilities of West Africa — particularly in gold, ivory, and slaves. The slave trade grew enormously between the 16th and 19th centuries, creating an atmosphere of fear and mistrust right across Africa that affected all later exploration of that vast continent.

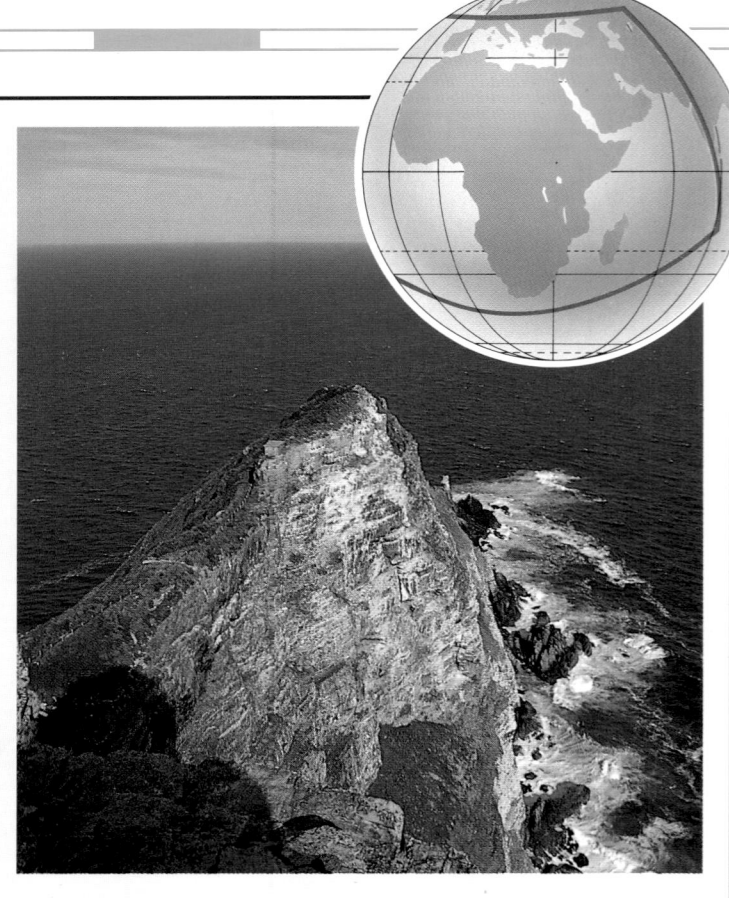

### Hope for the future

The rocky headland on the southwest tip of Africa was named the Cape of Storms by Bartolomeu Dias in 1487. But it was renamed the Cape of Good Hope by the Portuguese King John II, as it appeared to hold out the hope of a sea route to the Far East. Ten years passed before this sea route was confirmed by the Portuguese navigator Vasco da Gama, who rounded the Cape in 1497.

**Left** The Portuguese navigator Diogo Gomes reached the Gulf of Guinea in 1458, opening up the route for European traders. This carved door panel, made by the Yoruba people of Nigeria, shows a Portuguese trader on horseback.

**Right** Maps made in the middle of the 16th century could show the coasts of Africa in detail. By contrast, the interior of Africa was virtually unknown. The spokelike lines are an alternative to latitude and longitude: navigators could use them to work out their position.

**Right** The Portuguese progressed around Africa in a series of small steps, then giant leaps. The ultimate goal was always the spices of the East, but the travelers soon recognized the trading opportunities in Africa itself.

Eannes (1434)

Da Covilhã/Da Paiva (1487)

Da Covilhã (1487-90)

Dias (1487)

Da Gama (1497-99)

### Golden Guinea

Some West African countries became known by the most valuable trade goods found there. The British named a gold coin after the country from which the gold came: Guinea.

**Below** The Portuguese first set up trading posts along the coast of Africa, and then they built forts to protect them. The well-preserved thick walls of Fort Jesus in Mombasa, on the Kenyan coast of East Africa, show the typical architecture of Portuguese forts of the time.

**Right** When Vasco da Gama reached Mombasa in 1498 he was given a hostile reception, but was made welcome in Malindi, farther north. Here he managed to recruit Arab pilots to guide his ships to India (see pages 30-31) where he landed at Calicut in May of that year and found trade was controlled by Muslims.

**Left** The great rivers of Africa — such as the Niger — became a major theme of exploration in the 19th century. Mapmakers needed to know where these rivers began and ended — but that was an obsession that often puzzled local people.

# MAPPING THE RIVER NIGER

The west coast of Africa was famed for its riches in gold and ivory. Until the very end of the 18th century, however, all that European geographers knew of what lay beyond the coasts was that much of this wealth was traded along a great river called the Niger, and that the fabled city of Timbuktu lay on or near that river. Just where the River Niger flowed from and to remained a mystery. Some people even speculated that it might be attached to the River Nile.

In 1788 the Association for Promoting the Discovery of Interior Parts of Africa (the African Association for short) was founded by Sir Joseph Banks, the naturalist who had accompanied Captain Cook (see pages 74–75). Its main aim was to encourage scientific exploration in Africa. It set its sights on West Africa and the River Niger, and sent the explorer Mungo Park on two expeditions there in 1795 and 1805.

Mungo Park died when close to unraveling the mystery of the Niger. His work was only completed in 1830 when the British brothers Richard and John Lander traveled by canoe from Bussa to the mouth of the river. However, Park's courage, determination, scientific thoroughness, and kindliness became a model for 19th-century exploration which, sadly, few European explorers succeeded in living up to.

**Left** In the 1820s the Geographical Society of Paris offered a prize of 10,000 francs to the first person to reach Timbuktu — and return alive. A British army officer, Alexander Gordon Laing, reached it in 1826, but was murdered there. The prize was won by a Frenchman, René Caillié (1799–1838), who traveled from Senegal to Timbuktu in 1827–1828, disguised as an Egyptian Muslim. Then, to reach home, he crossed the Sahara with a camel caravan.

Timbuktu was a great disappointment to Caillié. He found little sign of the wealthy gold-trading center it once had been (see pages 42–43).

**Right** Djenné, in modern Mali, was founded on a tributary of the River Niger in the 8th century and grew into a wealthy trading town and an important center for Islamic learning.

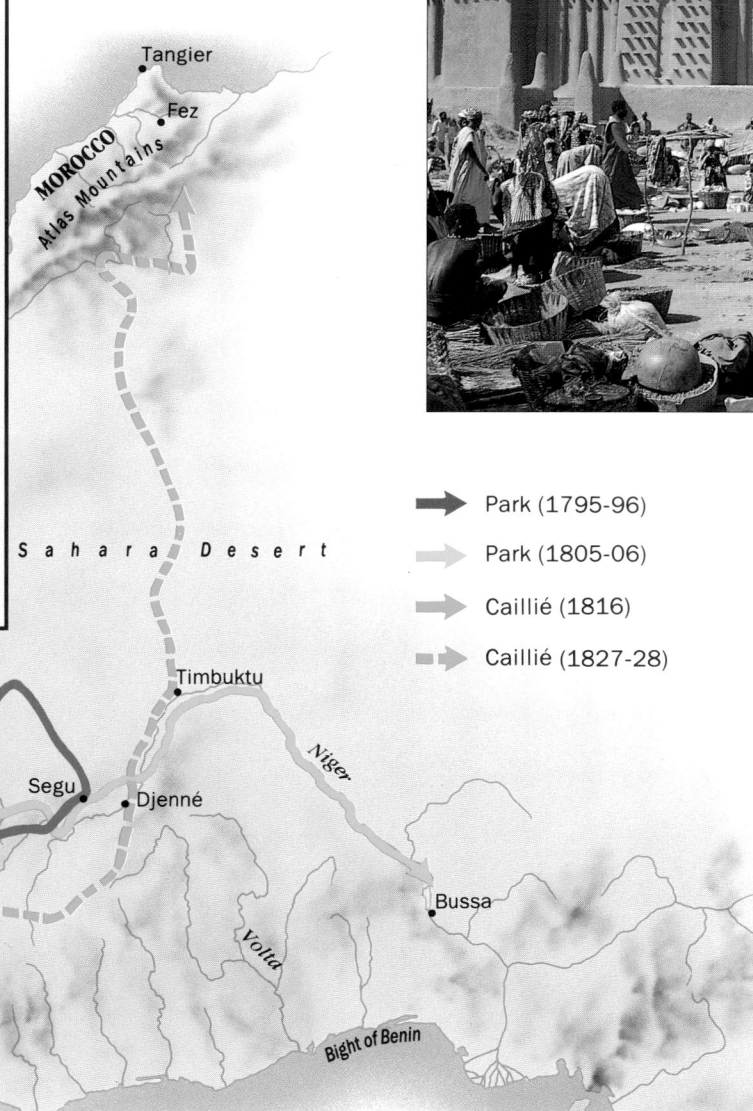

Tangier
Fez
MOROCCO
Atlas Mountains

Sahara Desert

Timbuktu

Segu
Djenné

Niger

Bussa

Volta

Cape Verde
Senegal

GAMBIA

ATLANTIC

OCEAN

SIERRA LEONE
Freetown

Bight of Benin

GULF OF GUINEA

➡ Park (1795-96)
➡ Park (1805-06)
➡ Caillié (1816)
➡ Caillié (1827-28)

## Heroism and tragedy

Mungo Park (1771–1806), a young Scottish doctor, was chosen by the African Association to undertake their first expedition to West Africa, to explore the River Niger. He set off from Gambia in 1795. Despite being abandoned by his African companions and imprisoned by Arabs for four months, he reached the Niger, and established that it flows eastward.

In 1805 Park returned to the Niger as leader of a large expedition. He traveled much of the length of the river, but the expedition was a disaster. Most of its members died of disease, and Park and the rest of his team were killed in an ambush at Bussa.

**Left** Explorers faced huge difficulties crossing the interior of West Africa. Tropical forest cloaks much of the landscape. After centuries of disruption by the slave trade, local tribes were constantly at war and often hostile, and Europeans had little defense against tropical diseases such as malaria and dysentery. West Africa soon became known as the "white man's grave," but this did not stop European governments from pressing for territorial expansion. By the 19th century the entire area was controlled by Britain, France, Germany, or Portugal.

**Above** Compared to the journeys of, say, Ibn Battuta in the 14th century (see pages 42-43), the achievements of the first European explorers in West Africa may look modest — but the distances covered are a measure of the extremely difficult conditions in which they traveled. These were, nonetheless, important early steps in the European exploration of the African interior.

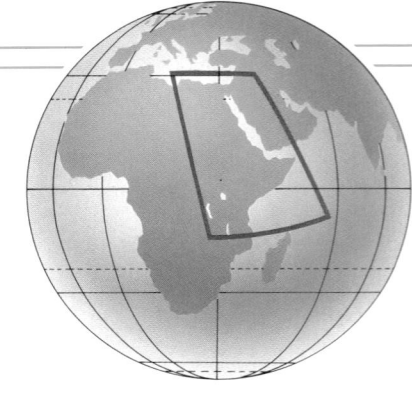

# THE SOURCE OF THE NILE

The great River Nile has been the subject of fascination since ancient times. But where did it flow from? How long was it? Ptolemy (see pages 10–11) suggested that it flowed from lakes in the "Mountains of the Moon" in East Africa. The Romans sent an expedition up the Nile, but they got only as far as the swamplands of modern-day southern Sudan which are known as the Sudd.

By the 1850s much of northern and western Africa had been visited by explorers such as the German Heinrich Barth (1821–1865), who from 1849 to 1855 traveled across the Sahara to West Africa on a British expedition. The source of the Nile, however, remained a tantalizing mystery that many explorers were anxious to solve.

In 1856 Richard Burton (see pages 36–37) set out from Zanzibar with John Hanning Speke (1827–1864) to try to solve this mystery. Speke reached Lake Victoria, which he declared to be the source of the Nile. But his observations did not prove this. In 1860–1862 Speke traveled again to Lake Victoria, this time with James Grant (1827–1892). Again their results were inconclusive.

They happened, by chance, to meet Samuel and Florence Baker, who were on their way up the Nile from Khartoum. Together they had covered almost the entire length of the Nile. But there was still uncertainty about an unexplored stretch of the river between Lake Victoria and Lake Albert. It was Henry Morton Stanley (see pages 52–53) who finally, after years of speculation, proved that Lake Victoria is indeed the source of the Nile.

## Burton and Speke

In 1856 Burton and Speke, both officers in the British Indian Army, were sent in search of the source of the River Nile by the Royal Geographical Society. After suffering great hardship and illness, they reached Lake Tanganyika in 1858. Speke then headed off alone and reached Lake N'yanza (right), which he renamed Lake Victoria after his queen. He was sure that this was the source of the Nile, but he failed to investigate it properly. This infuriated Burton, especially when, back in England, he found that Speke was being celebrated as the discoverer of the source of the River Nile.

After Speke's second expedition of 1860–1862, with Grant, Burton was still sure that Speke had not proved that Lake Victoria was the source of the Nile. In 1864 the Royal Geographical Society invited Burton and Speke to settle the issue in an open debate. However, Speke was mysteriously killed in a shooting accident the day before the debate was due to open.

**Above** The Nile is the longest river in the world at 4,160 miles (6,695 km). The White Nile flows from Lake Victoria and the shorter Blue Nile flows from Ethiopia. They come together at Khartoum, Sudan, to form one river. This picture shows the Nile as it flows past Elephantine Island near the First Cataract — one of a series of natural rock barriers on the river. Excavations on the island have revealed carvings and inscriptions that have helped historians build up an extensive picture of what life was like in ancient Egypt.

South of the Fifth Cataract is the confluence of the Blue and White Nile. The origin of the Blue Nile was discovered in 1613. The source of the White Nile was not discovered for almost another 250 years.

## A Scotsman in Africa

In 1763, James Bruce, a Scottish wine merchant, was appointed British consul in Algiers. During his five years there he studied Arabic before setting off on his travels. He journeyed to Cairo and then to Ethiopia. He traveled to the headstream of the Blue Nile before returning along the Nile to Egypt, and then back to Britain where, sadly, he was ignored.

**Left** Bruce's achievements in East Africa in 1768-1773 were sufficient to make the African Association turn its attention to West Africa in 1795. It was another 75 years before the explorers focused on the Nile again.

**Below** Samuel White Baker (1821–1893) was a wealthy traveler and game hunter. In 1861 he set off up the Nile from Cairo. He met Speke and Grant in Gondokoro, then in 1864 reached and named Lake Albert. He was accompanied on his Nile expedition by his young Hungarian wife, Florence, whom he had bought in a Turkish slave market in Bulgaria.

## The fly in the ointment

The European expeditions into Africa became increasingly ambitious in the late 19th century, and explorers traveled with an enormous quantity of baggage. They took clothes, tents and camp beds, food and cooking equipment, navigational instruments, arms and ammunition, and gifts for the African chiefs they encountered during their expeditions.

In other parts of the world they might have used horses or mules. In East Africa this was not possible because the tsetse fly spreads a disease that kills pack animals. Instead, porters were hired to carry the equipment.

# EXPLORING THE HEART OF AFRICA

**Below** In 1855 Livingstone became the first European to set eyes on the mighty Victoria Falls on the River Zambezi.

Up until the 1850s, very little was known about the interior of Africa by the world outside. Various European nations had well-established trading stations and settlements on the coasts, but the rest was uncharted territory.

The Scottish missionary David Livingstone began his journey into the heart of Africa in 1849, when he traveled north from southern Africa across the Kalahari Desert and reached Lake Ngami. Between 1853 and 1856 he walked right across Africa. In 1865 he was sent by the Royal Geographical Society to look for the source of the Nile, which was still disputed despite Speke's discoveries. In 1866, however, he disappeared around Lake Nyasa (now Lake Malawi) and there were no reports of him for three years.

In 1871 the journalist Henry Morton Stanley succeeded in finding him, sick but alive. This famous meeting inspired Stanley to make two more major expeditions in Africa between 1874 and 1889.

Following in the footsteps of the explorers, almost all the European nations began to claim territory in Africa, justifying their action by stating that Africans would benefit from education and Christianity. Few people in Europe saw any wrong in this. Mary Kingsley, however, objected strongly. In 1895 she completed an extraordinarily courageous journey in western Africa, and her experiences led her to believe that traditional African ways of life should be respected and not interfered with. She was pointing the way toward the more sensitive kinds of exploration and anthropology of the 20th century, but her views were not accepted at the time.

### Explorer with a mission

David Livingstone (1813–1873) was a trained doctor and a Christian missionary. He was sent to South Africa in 1841, and he believed himself called to take the Gospel to tribes living in the lands to the north. By opening up the interior of Africa to missionary work and different forms of trade, he hoped to put an end to slavery — a point made clear by the title page of a biography (right) published in 1878. Through his goodwill, he won the affection and loyalty of his

African companions. After his death from dysentery near Lake Tanganyika, two of them carried his body nearly 1,000 miles (1,600 km) to Zanzibar so that it could be shipped to London. In Britain he was buried in Westminster Abbey and was mourned as a national hero.

Livingstone made detailed records of his travels, including a sketch map of his idea of the sources of the Nile. His maps and journals were extremely valuable to European geographers, who had few other sources of information about the region.

## Alone among cannibals

Mary Kingsley (1862–1900) made two journeys to the west coast of Africa in 1893 and 1895. She earned fame for her journey among the hostile Fang people, winning their respect by showing bravery and by interesting them in trading goods, such as fishhooks, knives, and cloth.

**Below** Livingstone and Stanley explored and mapped much of the interior of southern Africa over three decades. Mary Kingsley's journeys were on a much less grand scale.

**Above** The journeys of Livingstone and Stanley caught the public's imagination, as this Victorian board game shows. It paints a colorful but unrealistic picture.

## The workhouse boy

Henry Morton Stanley (1841–1904) started life in a workhouse for the poor in Wales. His real name was John Rowlands. When still a boy he ran away to the United States. He was adopted by a wealthy man called Henry Morton Stanley, and he changed his name in his benefactor's honor. He became a successful journalist, and in 1871 he was sent by the editor of the *New York Herald* to discover what had happened to David Livingstone, whose exploits had captured the imagination of the American public. This was the start of his life as an explorer.

In 1874 he traveled from Zanzibar to Lake Victoria and proved that this was the source of the River Nile. He continued westward, sailing down the River Lualaba and the River Congo (now Zaire), reaching the west coast after a journey lasting 999 days. He led one further expedition, to southern Sudan, in 1887–1889.

All of Stanley's expeditions were on an enormous scale, involving hundreds of guides and porters traveling long distances in very hazardous conditions. When he crossed Africa in 1874–1877, for example, Stanley set out with 356 people; only 115 of these reached the west coast.

→ Livingstone (1841-73)

⇢ Stanley (1871)

➡ Stanley (1874-77)

➡ Kingsley (1895)

Libreville

Ogowe

Congo (Zaire)

Boma

Lualaba

Lake Victoria

Ujiji   Tabora

Lake Tanganyika

ZANZIBAR

Dar es Salaam

*ATLANTIC*

*OCEAN*

*INDIAN OCEAN*

Lake Bangweulu

Lake Nyasa

*Zambezi*

Lake Ngami

*Limpopo*

**Kalahari Desert**

*Orange*

Cape Town

**Above** Stanley found Livingstone in the village of Ujiji, near Lake Tanganyika. After a grueling journey lasting 10 months, he greeted Livingstone with the phrase: "Dr. Livingstone, I presume."

# SECTION 5: THE AMERICAS

The first Europeans arrived in South and Central America in 1492. They quickly realized this "New World" offered land to conquer and to claim for themselves. For the people already living there, European exploration was to bring tragedy and destruction.

## MOVING SOUTH

The first inhabitants of America crossed over from Asia around 25,000 years ago. When a corridor opened up to the east of the Rocky Mountains at the end of the last Ice Age around 12,000 years ago, they pushed down toward the temperate plains of North America and the warmer and much more hospitable lands farther south.

North America was inhabited mainly by farmers and semi-nomadic hunters, while town-building civilizations developed in Central America as early as 1000 BC. The Mayas came to rule much of Central America until their Empire collapsed about AD 900, when the Toltecs became dominant. They in turn were pushed out in the 13th century by the Aztecs when they invaded the Valley of Mexico.

Meanwhile, in the Andes Mountains of South America, several early civilizations developed, and in the 15th century they were brought under the rule of the Incas.

**Above** The ancestors of the North American Indians were nomadic hunters. Gradually their lives became settled, and by 1000 BC most tribes grew much of their own food by farming the river valleys. Hunting remained an important part of life for many groups, however.

**Below** All the cultures of Central and South America built palaces and temples on a massive scale, often with giant sculptures to match. The Olmecs, who dominated Central America from 1200 to 400 BC, made huge stone heads using hammers made of very hard stone.

### Making their mark

The territories of the Adena and Hopewell Indians of the central eastern part of North America were marked by huge mounds of earth which served as burial sites or as platforms for temples. Some mounds have precise geometric shapes; others represent animals such as birds or snakes, such as those at the Serpent Mound in Ohio (above).

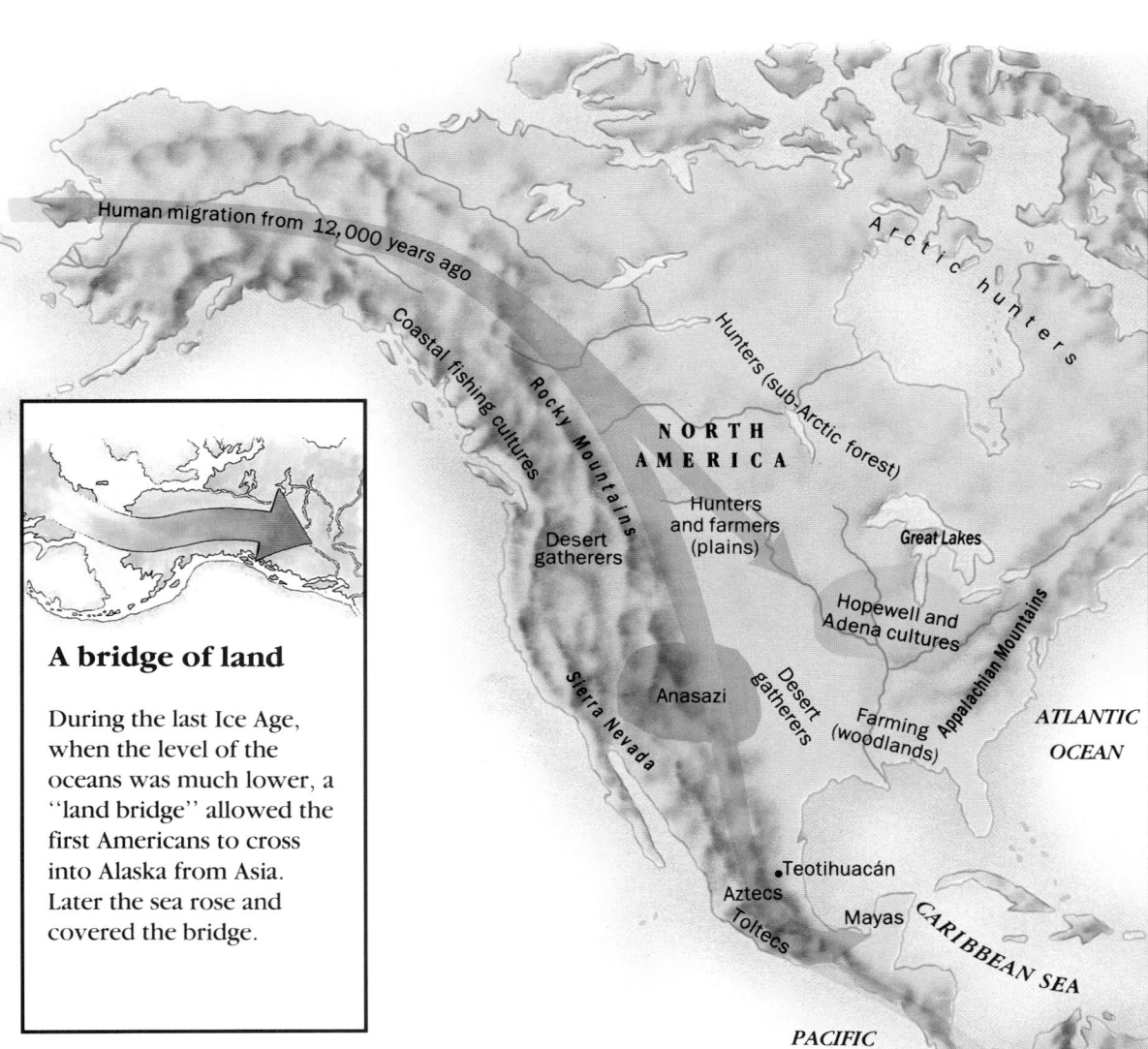

Human migration from 12,000 years ago

Coastal fishing cultures

Rocky Mountains

Arctic hunters

Hunters (sub-Arctic forest)

**NORTH AMERICA**

Desert gatherers

Hunters and farmers (plains)

Great Lakes

Hopewell and Adena cultures

Sierra Nevada

Anasazi

Desert gatherers

Farming (woodlands)

Appalachian Mountains

**ATLANTIC OCEAN**

Teotihuacán

Aztecs

Toltecs

Mayas

**CARIBBEAN SEA**

**PACIFIC OCEAN**

Farmers (rain forest and savannah)

**SOUTH AMERICA**

Andes Mountains

Incas

Cuzco

Tiahuanaco

Hunters (grasslands and savannah)

Fishing cultures

## A bridge of land

During the last Ice Age, when the level of the oceans was much lower, a "land bridge" allowed the first Americans to cross into Alaska from Asia. Later the sea rose and covered the bridge.

## The golden touch

The people of the Andes were gifted craftsmen, with a unique way of portraying the world — as demonstrated by this pottery whistling bottle showing a man playing the Andean panpipes. They were also famous for their immense riches in gold, which they cast and sculpted into jewelry, ornaments, and tools.

**Above** The Aztecs' colorful clothes and jewelry may have impressed the first European visitors, but the Aztecs lacked glass, iron, gunpowder, and even the wheel.

**Below** By about AD 400 the Anasazi of southwest North America were living in villages built of stone or adobe (mud bricks). Later settlements were concealed in cliffs.

**Above** The first inhabitants of the Americas lived in the Arctic until the withdrawal of the ice cap 12,000 years ago allowed them to cross into the rest of North America. By about 2000 BC farming cultures were established.

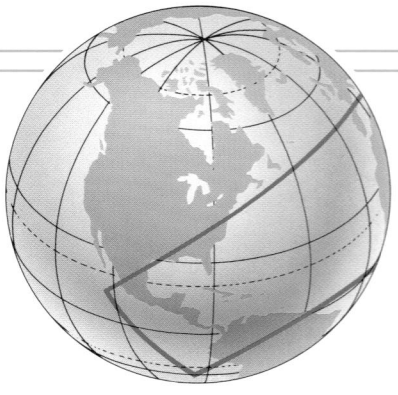

# EUROPEAN ARRIVAL

In 1492 three small Spanish ships, the *Santa Maria*, the *Niña*, and the *Pinta*, arrived on a tiny island in the Bahamas. The leader of the expedition, Christopher Columbus, named the island San Salvador (Holy Savior). The ships were carrying the first Europeans to reach the Caribbean. This was the first of a new wave of European expeditions which would soon change the Americas forever.

The Portuguese had been searching for a route to the Far East by pushing south down the coast of Africa. Columbus, by contrast, thought that it should be possible to reach the East by sailing westward across the Atlantic. This is what Ptolemy's map (see pages 10–11) suggested. Unfortunately Ptolemy had underestimated the circumference of the world. When Columbus reached San Salvador, he thought he had reached the Far East, and that the riches of China and India lay close by. He called the people living there "Indians," and the islands the "Indies." This misnomer has persisted ever since.

Columbus made three more voyages, in 1493–1496, 1498–1500, and 1502–1504, visiting and naming many of the islands of the Caribbean, as well as the coasts of South and Central America. However, he never found the great quantities of gold he had dreamed of, and he never understood fully that he had not reached the Far East.

**Right**
This map, dated 1500, was drawn by Juan de la Cosa, who was with Columbus on his second voyage. It shows that most of the Caribbean had already been carefully charted by this time. St. Christopher, Columbus's patron saint, is pictured with his head pointing toward the riches of the East.

### Hero and villain

Christopher Columbus, or Cristóbal Colón (1451–1506), was a weaver's son from Genoa in Italy. He was in the service of the Portuguese for about 10 years, but when the Portuguese king refused to support his plan to cross the Atlantic, he turned to King Ferdinand and Queen Isabella of Spain for assistance.

He was treated as a hero when he returned to Spain from his first expedition, and was made governor of the

## By the stars above

Christopher Columbus would undoubtedly have used a compass in his voyages across the Atlantic. Another instrument he would have used was the quadrant, which was a flat piece of wood or metal shaped like a quarter circle. A scale was drawn around the edge and when the instrument was held upright the navigator could work out a star's height above the horizon. A ship's position could be worked out by using a star chart.

**Left** "Gold, God and Cathay (China)" were the reasons why Columbus wanted to reach the Far East. Queen Isabella of Spain was particularly attracted to the idea that Columbus would take Christianity to the people of the East. One of his first acts in San Salvador was to raise a cross.

**Below** Columbus's four voyages all led him to the same region of the Caribbean. They became progressively less rewarding as he ran into problems of colonization and administration. He remained convinced that he had discovered the Far East.

Columbus's four voyages

➡ First voyage (1492-93)

➡ Second voyage (1493-96)

➡ Third voyage (1498-1500)

➡ Fourth voyage (1502-04)

new islands that he had discovered. But he was clearly unsuited to these responsibilities. On later expeditions he treated the Spanish settlers cruelly. He also forced the Indians to give up their gold, and sent many of them to Spain as slaves. On his third voyage in 1498 he was arrested and sent home to Spain in chains.

Queen Isabella gave him one more chance, sending him on a fourth voyage in 1502 to look for a strait that might connect the Caribbean

Sea to the Pacific Ocean. The expedition was a disaster: his ships became unseaworthy with marine worms, and Columbus had to be rescued from Jamaica. He returned to Spain a broken, bitter man.

**Right** The "Cathedral Primada de America" in Santo Domingo was completed in 1540. More than 300 years later, Columbus's remains were interred there.

# CLAIMING THE NEW WORLD

Before Columbus's death in 1506, Spain had established a major colony on Hispaniola, and both the Spanish and the Portuguese had begun to explore the coasts of Central and South America in search of gold and new territories to colonize.

To prevent unnecessary squabbles, in 1494 Spain and Portugal signed the Treaty of Tordesillas. A line was drawn down the world at 370 leagues (about 1,250 miles [2,000 km]) to the west of the Cape Verde Islands. Any newly discovered territories to the west of the line would be Spanish, and any to the east would be Portuguese.

Brazil was discovered by accident by the Portuguese navigator Pedro Álvares Cabral in 1500. He named the area he discovered "Land of the True Cross." Since it was to the east of the line of Tordesillas, Portugal could claim it. The remainder of South America was later claimed by Spain.

There was little attempt to explore the interior of the new continent for the time being. In 1513, however, Vasco Núñez de Balboa crossed the isthmus of Central America in Panama and became the first European to see the Pacific Ocean, which he promptly claimed for Spain.

**Left** Navigational tools remained simple throughout this period. Windroses such as this helped navigators to plot the course of their ship by recording the direction, strength, and frequency of the wind.

**Below** Fernandez de Córdoba reached the Yucatán peninsula in 1517, and became the first European to see remains of the Mayan civilization, such as the spectacular pyramid at Tikal in Guatemala. He was followed by Juan de Grijalva in 1518, who was the first European to learn of the Aztecs.

**Left** The early explorers came across all kinds of animals and plants that were new to them. Artists attempting to illustrate their tales back at home often misunderstood what was being described to them. This is why these flying fish appear to be soaring like birds among the ship's rigging.

## Fruits of exploration

A number of plants and foods that are familiar to us today were seen by Europeans for the first time in the Caribbean. Columbus was the first to report on the pineapple. Potato, maize (corn), and tobacco are all originally Taino (Arawak) words. The Arawaks used to smoke rolled-up tobacco leaves through their nostrils, much to the alarm and amusement of the explorers and the disbelief of those they told this to on their return to Europe.

European sailors slept on the deck before they discovered the comfortable hanging beds which the Arawaks called hammocks. Other English words that probably come from the Taino language include canoe, cannibal, hurricane, and barbecue.

**Right** Cabral, Vespucci, and others began to acquire an understanding of the scale of the landmass of South America. The exploration of the Americas, however, was to follow from the voyages of Balboa and Córdoba.

## The United States of Americus!

Amerigo Vespucci (1454–1512) was an Italian from Florence who was posted to Spain as an agent for a bank. He took great interest in exploration and supported Columbus on his first voyage. In 1499 he joined an expedition that explored the mouth of the Amazon, and in 1501–1502 he sailed down much of the east coast of South America. Unlike Columbus, he was convinced that this coast was not part of the Far East, but belonged to a continent he called the New World.

In 1508, Vespucci was appointed Pilot Major (examiner of ships' pilots) — a position he held till he died in 1512.

When Martin Waldseemüller, the noted geographer, produced a new map of the world in 1507, he proposed that this new continent should be called America, after Vespucci's Latinized name, Americus Vespuccius.

However, by 1513 Waldseemüller felt that Vespucci's contribution had not been so great after all. Too late: the name America had been accepted.

NORTH AMERICA

FLORIDA

GULF OF MEXICO

SARGASSO SEA

CUBA

HISPANIOLA

YUCATAN

• Tikal   CARIBBEAN SEA

ATLANTIC OCEAN

PANAMA

Amazon

CABO SÃO ROQUE

B R A Z I L

SOUTH AMERICA

PACIFIC OCEAN

• Rio de Janeiro

Line of the Treaty of Tordesillas, 1494

Plate

Vespucci (1499)
Cabral (1500)
Vespucci (1501-02)

Balboa (1513)
Córdoba (1517)
Grijalva (1518)

# CIRCUMNAVIGATION

In the first two decades of the 16th century the Spanish had seen the "Southern Ocean" (the Pacific) from Central America, and the Portuguese had seen it from Southeast Asia (see pages 30–31). What lay between these two points was a mystery that many explorers were eager to solve.

The big question was still whether there was a sea route to the East across or around the Americas. This was particularly important to Spain. If the route could be found, Spain might be able to reach and claim some of the Spice Islands under the Treaty of Tordesillas (see pages 58–59).

In 1519 Ferdinand Magellan, a Portuguese captain working for Spain, was sent to find out. He found a passage around the southern tip of South America. He named the sea beyond this the Pacific ("peaceful") Ocean because it was so calm.

Magellan was killed in the Philippines, and by this time the Spice Islands had been claimed by the Portuguese. But all was not lost: Magellan's expedition could claim to be the first ever to sail around (or circumnavigate) the world.

It was over 50 years before this feat was repeated, by Francis Drake.

## Half the way around

Ferdinand Magellan (about 1480–1521) was an experienced navigator who had accompanied Afonso de Albuquerque's expedition to Southeast Asia in 1511 (see pages 30–31). When the king of Portugal refused to send him on further expeditions, he turned to the king of Spain. He proposed to find a route that would allow Spain to reach the Spice Islands by sailing from east to west. In 1519 he set off for South America with five ships and a crew of 241 men. In 1520 his ships sailed through the strait at the tip of South America (above) now called after him. Halfway around the world, there was a skirmish on the island of Mactan and Magellan was killed.

The surviving members of the expedition continued under the leadership of Juan Sebastián del Cano. In the end only one ship, the *Victoria*, reached Spain in 1522. On board were 18 of the men who had sailed from Spain in 1519.

**Left** This map of 1578 shows Tierra del Fuego attached to an unknown southern continent *terra incognita*, based on Magellan's observations. It was Drake's expedition of 1577–1580 that established Tierra del Fuego as an island by sailing to its south, through what is now known as Drake Passage. Drake sailed up the Pacific coast of South America to plunder Spanish settlements there. By the time he reached England his holds were laden with silver, gold, spices, and porcelain, which he presented to Queen Elizabeth I, who promptly knighted him.

## "The Dragon"

The English captain Francis Drake (about 1540–1596) was a brilliant navigator, but to the Spanish he was little more than a pirate. After the repeated success of his raids against Spanish settlements in the Caribbean and Central America, they called him "El Draco," the Dragon.

In 1577 Drake, with the approval of Queen Elizabeth I, set off on a voyage of exploration to the southern seas. By the time he reached the Pacific Ocean three of his ships had been lost, and one had returned to England, but Drake continued on the *Golden Hind* (right) and raided Valparaíso and Lima. Searching for a strait that would lead back to the Atlantic, he landed in northern California, which he named New Albion and claimed for England. He then headed westward and completed his circumnavigation in 1580.

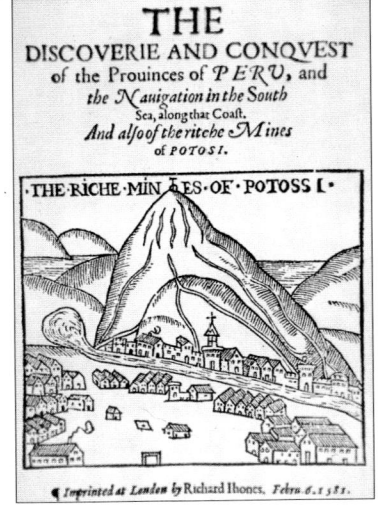

**Above** Both Magellan's and Drake's expeditions followed more or less the same course. Magellan's expedition came close to disaster when it was becalmed in the southeast Pacific. Drake avoided the region by sailing up the west coast of the Americas.

**Left** The town of Potosí, in southern Bolivia, was founded by the Spanish in 1546 around a rich silver mine. In 1579 Drake attacked and plundered a ship loaded with Potosí silver.

### Survival rations

One of the survivors of Magellan's expedition was the Italian Antonio Pigafetta. He wrote a famous account of the journey, in which he described some of the terrible hardships endured by the crew. They came close to starvation in the eastern Pacific, and only survived by drinking foul water, and eating sawdust, leather, and rotting biscuits such as this, which were often contaminated by rats' droppings.

Map labels: ARCTIC OCEAN, GREENLAND, NORTH AMERICA, EUROPE, ASIA, PACIFIC OCEAN, CHINA, INDIA, AZORES, ATLANTIC OCEAN, CAPE VERDE ISLANDS, AFRICA, PHILIPPINE ISLANDS, MACTAN, INDIAN OCEAN, San Francisco Bay, CARIBBEAN SEA, SOUTH AMERICA, Lima, Potosí, Recife, Rio de Janeiro, Valparaíso, MARQUESAS ISLANDS, AUSTRALIA, NEW ZEALAND, Strait of Magellan, TIERRA DEL FUEGO, Drake Passage

Legend:
Magellan (1519-21)
Del Cano (1521-22)
Drake (1577-80)

# THE CONQUISTADORS

In 1519 Hernán Cortés (1485–1547) was appointed by the Spanish governor of Cuba to lead an expedition to "New Spain" (Mexico), which Juan de Grijalva had visited the year before. Cortés was a "conquistador," a warrior in pursuit of conquest in the name of Spain and Christianity.

He landed in New Spain with only 600 men, but he quickly made alliances with various Indian peoples, such as the Totonacs and Tlaxcaltecs, who did not like being ruled by the Aztecs. At Tenochtitlán, the Aztec capital, they found the Aztecs in a state of confusion, and Cortés succeeded in taking hostage their leader, Montezuma. After a series of bitter squabbles and battles, the Spanish and their Indian allies laid siege to Tenochtitlán and in 1521 the Aztecs were defeated. Within five years Cortés had control of the whole of the Aztec Empire.

Cortés was never appointed viceroy of Mexico as he had hoped. He was created Marquis del Valle de Oaxaca. After his death in Spain, his remains were returned to Mexico.

Cortés's daring conquest set the tone for the next great feat of the conquistadors: the conquest of Peru in 1532 by Francisco Pizarro.

South America was changed forever — by conquest, and also by European diseases. The population of South America in 1519 has been estimated at 57 million; in 1607 it was 4 million.

**Above** Hernán Cortés brought a new level of ruthlessness to the Spanish conquest of the Americas that caused offense in Spain even in his own day. He died in Spain in 1547, resentful that his achievements had not been properly acknowledged.

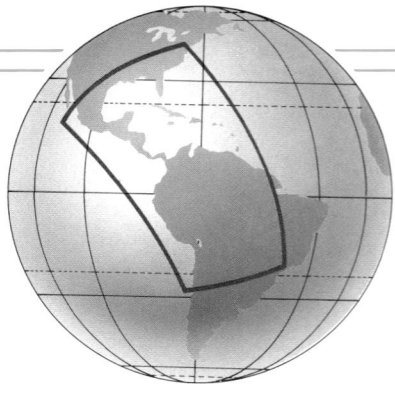

## The Mendoza Codex

The Aztecs compiled books written in pictures, called *codices*, which tell us what life was like in Aztec times. In the 16th century, when the Spanish were firmly in control of Mexico, the governor, Antonio de Mendoza, ordered a codex to be made for the king of Spain to show him what life was like in Mexico at the time. This is one of the pages from the Mendoza Codex.

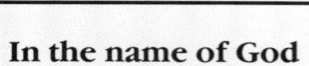

**Below** A group of monumental cities such as this one, Teotihuacán, surrounded the Aztec capital Tenochtitlán. It was at Tenochtitlán that Cortés finally forced the Aztecs to submit to Spanish rule when Cuauhtemac surrendered the city to the Spanish conquistador. He went on to conquer Honduras, and his armies took control of Guatemala and El Salvador.

## In the name of God

Francisco Pizarro (1476–1541) had heard rumors of the gold of the Incas in 1513 when he accompanied Balboa's expedition across Central America (see pages 58–59). After Cortés's conquest of the Aztecs, Pizarro became determined to conquer the Incas.

His first attempts in 1524 and 1526 failed, but in 1532 he reached Peru with just 185 men and 27 horses. They found the Inca Empire

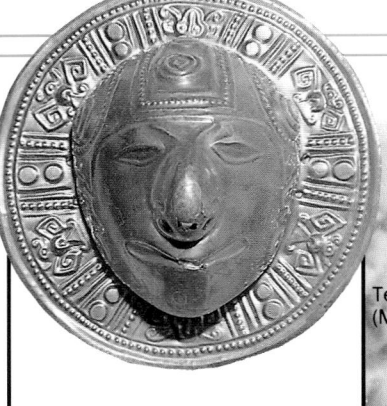

## Eldorado

The Spanish found vast quantities of gold such as this mask in South America, particularly in Colombia and Peru. Many conquistadors were inspired to press farther into unexplored regions by the legend of the Golden Man, "El Dorado," the ruler of a land of gold. The possible location of the land of Eldorado moved as each region was explored, and it was never found.

**Below** The conquistadors destroyed the great empires of Central and South America with extraordinarily small forces. The Spanish had several important advantages: they had gunpowder and firearms, armor and horses, all of which terrified their opposition, who had none of these.

**Below** Both Cortés and Pizarro traveled fairly short distances to reach the heart of civilizations previously unknown to them. Their expeditions could be described as conquest rather than exploration.

GULF OF MEXICO

BAHAMAS

CUBA

HISPANIOLA

JAMAICA

GULF OF HONDURAS

CARIBBEAN SEA

Tenochtitlán (Mexico City)

Veracruz

Panama

Quito

SOUTH AMERICA

Marañon

Tangaiaia

Cajamarca

Ucayali

Santa

Lima

Machu Picchu

Cuzco

Lake Titicaca

Andes Mountains

→ Cortés (1519)

→ Pizarro (1531-32)

→ Pizarro (1533)

on the verge of civil war, as two princes, Atahualpa and Huáscar, contested the throne. Pizarro exploited this situation. He invited Atahualpa to a meeting in Cajamarca. But it was a trick: when Atahualpa rejected the offer to become Christian, the Spanish massacred the Incas and captured Atahualpa.

To win his freedom, the Incas had to fill a large room with gold and silver. Meanwhile Atahualpa managed to arrange the assassination of Huáscar.

Atahualpa was tried by the Spanish and executed for murder. The Inca Empire fell into chaos, and Pizarro was able to march into its capital, Cuzco. However, the Spanish then squabbled among themselves, and Pizarro himself was murdered by rivals in 1541.

**Right** Machu Picchu, an Inca fortress and settlement high up in the Andes, lay forgotten for centuries until it was rediscovered in 1911.

# SCIENTIFIC EXPLORATION

Several of the Spanish conquistadors in the 16th and early 17th century took the search for Eldorado over the Andes and into the interior of South America. In 1542 Francisco de Orellana traveled down much of the Amazon. An encounter with one tribe reminded him of the women warriors called Amazons in ancient Greek legend — so the river gained its name.

The huge advances in science over the next two centuries, however, brought a new kind of explorer to South America: the scientist in search of knowledge. One of the greatest of these was the German geologist and naturalist Baron Alexander von Humboldt. From 1799–1804 he explored much of the Orinoco River. Then he traveled through the northern Andes to Peru. His painstaking methods of research set the standard for all scientific expeditions that followed, including the one that was to have the most profound effect on people's understanding of their own evolution.

From 1831–1836 the British naturalist Charles Darwin sailed around the coasts of South America on board HMS *Beagle* — a voyage that was to result in a radical change in the way people understood the world.

Three British scientists, Alfred Russell Wallace, Henry Bates, and Richard Spruce,

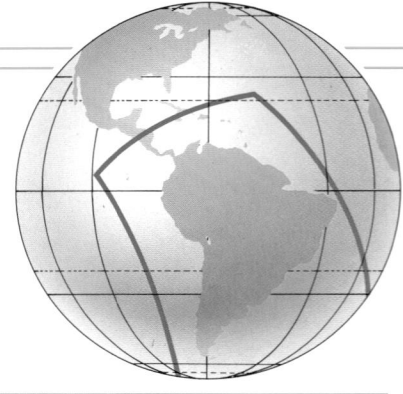

**Below** The Galápagos Islands lie on the Equator, 680 miles (1,100 km) to the west of South America. Ecuador took possession of them in 1832, three years before the *Beagle* anchored in their waters.

spent a combined total of 32 years in the Amazon region from 1848 on, and collected thousands of specimens of plants, insects, and other animals. They suffered from malaria and dysentery, and faced constant danger from turbulent rivers, alligators, and snakes — all for the cause of science.

## Scientist and hero

Alexander von Humboldt (1769–1859) was an energetic scientist who made observations about everything he came upon — geology, geography, climate, botany, people. He traveled with a large set of scientific instruments, collected thousands of specimens, and made detailed notes. His sketches formed the basis for the illustrations, such as this balsa raft on the Orinoco River, used in popular accounts of his journeys.

In South America he was accompanied by the French doctor Aimé Bonpland (1773–1858). They carried out numerous experiments, often at great risk to themselves. During an earthquake, for example, Humboldt calmly set about measuring the electricity in the atmosphere. In just five years they traveled about 40,000 miles (64,000 km), and returned home with 335 cases of specimens.

Back in Europe Humboldt was treated as a hero and was honored by many institutions. He devoted his last years to writing.

## Descended from the apes

Charles Darwin (1809–1882) was only 22 years old when he joined HMS *Beagle* for its five-year voyage around South America. It took him another 23 years to produce the book that explained his new theory of evolution. *On the Origin of Species by Means of Natural Selection* was published in 1859. Darwin's ideas were considered revolutionary at the time. They appeared to contradict the Bible, which said the world had been created by God in six days. In his book *The Descent of Man*, published in 1871, he took the idea one step further by suggesting that the human species was descended from apes.

Despite the alarm these new ideas caused, Darwin was celebrated as a major figure of his day, and many of his ideas were quickly adopted.

**Right** Humboldt and Darwin, as well as scientists working in the Amazon Basin, revealed the immense riches of South America, but they covered only a small part of its vast area. Despite increasing amounts of land being taken over for farming and ranching, large areas still remain virtually unexplored today.

→ Humboldt and Bonpland (1799-1800)
⇢ Humboldt and Bonpland (1801-1803)
→ Darwin (1831-35)

## A world of its own

Darwin noticed that the wildlife on the Galápagos Islands had adapted over many generations to the special conditions on the islands. For instance, finches such as the ones above had evolved different-shaped beaks according to whether they ate nuts, insects, or fruit. Colonies of giant tortoises, living in isolation on various islands, had developed in different ways. (*Galápago* means "tortoise" in Spanish.)

Such observations helped Darwin to form his ideas on evolution based on what he called "natural selection." The animals that survive are the ones that have the features best suited to their environment. They are the most likely to breed successfully and pass these features on.

CARIBBEAN
SEA

Cartagena
Caracas
Orinoco

Quito
Llanos

GALAPAGOS
ISLANDS

Amazon

SOUTH
AMERICA

Lima

BRAZIL

Bahia (Salvador)

Mato Grosso Plateau

PACIFIC
OCEAN

Rio de Janeiro

Paraná

Valparaíso

Pampas

Montevideo

Buenos Aires

ATLANTIC
OCEAN

Strait of
Magellan

# EASTERN NORTH AMERICA

The east coast of North America had been visited by Vikings around AD1000 (see pages 16–17), but these experiences had been all but forgotten by the 15th century. When the Italian navigator John Cabot sailed from Bristol, England, in 1497 and reached Newfoundland, he thought that it was China.

The search then began for the Northwest Passage — a route to the East around the north coast of Canada. This led the French navigator Jacques Cartier up the St. Lawrence River in 1534. Martin Frobisher made several efforts to find the Northwest Passage from 1576 to 1578; likewise John Davis in 1585–1587, Henry Hudson in 1609–1611, William Baffin and Robert Bylot in 1615 and 1616 — all of them failed to find the Passage and many began to wonder if it existed at all.

The search for the Northwest Passage overshadowed the opportunities offered by North America itself. Several attempts were made to set up colonies, by the Portuguese in the 1520s, the French and Spanish in the 1560s, and the English in the 1580s and 1590s, but little came of them.

In 1603, however, the French explorer Samuel de Champlain (1567–1635) traveled up the St. Lawrence River to look for land to settle. He founded Quebec in 1608, and both Dutch and English settlements along the east coast followed soon after.

**Below** Frobisher met the Inuit on his first voyage of 1576. Although contact with them was initially friendly, the Inuit abducted five of his crew. Frobisher responded by seizing an Inuit couple.

## From east to west

French and British fur traders and trappers were responsible for much of the exploration of the continent during the 17th and 18th centuries. Alexander Mackenzie (about 1764–1820) was a Scottish fur trader who worked for the North West Company. Mackenzie was interested in opening up a route that would lead across Canada to the Pacific. In 1789, accompanied by an Indian chief and several French Canadians with their Indian wives, he followed a river from Lake Athabasca. Unfortunately this led northwest to flow into the Arctic Ocean. The river is now named after him.

In 1792–1793 he led a similar party along the Peace River and then down part of the Fraser River to reach the Pacific and become the first recorded European to cross North America north of Mexico.

**Above** The Inuit, or Eskimos, were found across the northern coast of Canada, as well as in Alaska and Siberia. Living by hunting and trapping, they offered valuable trade in furs and walrus ivory. Some early explorers in search of the Northwest Passage thought that the Asian features of the Inuit meant that China was not far off. The Inuit were also skilled whalers, as we can see from this carving on a walrus-ivory show knife of the 19th century.

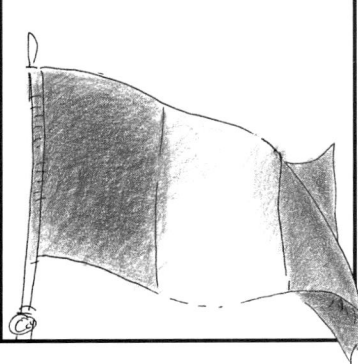

Map labels:

GREENLAND
BAFFIN BAY
BAFFIN ISLAND
Davis Strait
Cumberland Sound
FOXE BASIN
Hudson Strait
Mackenzie
HUDSON BAY
LABRADOR
LABRADOR SEA
Peace
Lake Athabasca
C A N A D A
Nelson
QUEBEC
St. Lawrence
NEWFOUNDLAND
Lake Superior
Quebec
Montreal
Lake Michigan
Lake Huron
Lake Ontario
Lake Erie
NOVA SCOTIA
Port Royal
Cape Cod
Appalachian Mountains
LOUISIANA
Mississippi
GULF OF MEXICO

Legend:

- - -▸ Cabot (1497)
- - -▸ Cartier (1534)
——▸ Cartier (1535-36)
——▸ Frobisher (1576-78)
- - ▸ Davis (1585-87)
——▸ Champlain (1603-15)
- - ▸ Hudson (1610)
——▸ Bylot and Baffin (1615)
- - ▸ Bylot and Baffin (1616)
——▸ La Salle (1679-1682)

**Left** Many of the place names of the Canadian north are memorials to the explorers who struggled in vain to find a Northwest Passage to the East. Only after Europeans had settled successfully in these lands in the early 1600s did explorers begin to press on into the interior.

## Louisiana

In 1679 the French explorer Robert de La Salle (1643–1687) set off from the Great Lakes to pioneer a trade route southward across the heart of North America. He traveled down the Mississippi River to the Gulf of Mexico, setting up trading forts along the way. He declared the vast territory he had covered to be French and called it Louisiana, in honor of his king, Louis XIV.

## Abandoned at sea

Henry Hudson made three journeys to the northern seas in search of a passage to the East. In 1609, sailing for the Dutch East India Company, he explored much of the east coast of North America. In 1610, sponsored by English merchants, he reached Hudson Bay. Forced to spend a grueling winter there, his crew mutinied and put him in a boat with his son and loyal members of the crew. They were never seen again. Hudson's name is recalled by the bay, in the Hudson River and Mountains, in the two towns named after him, and also by the Hudson's Bay Company, which did much to open up huge areas of North America.

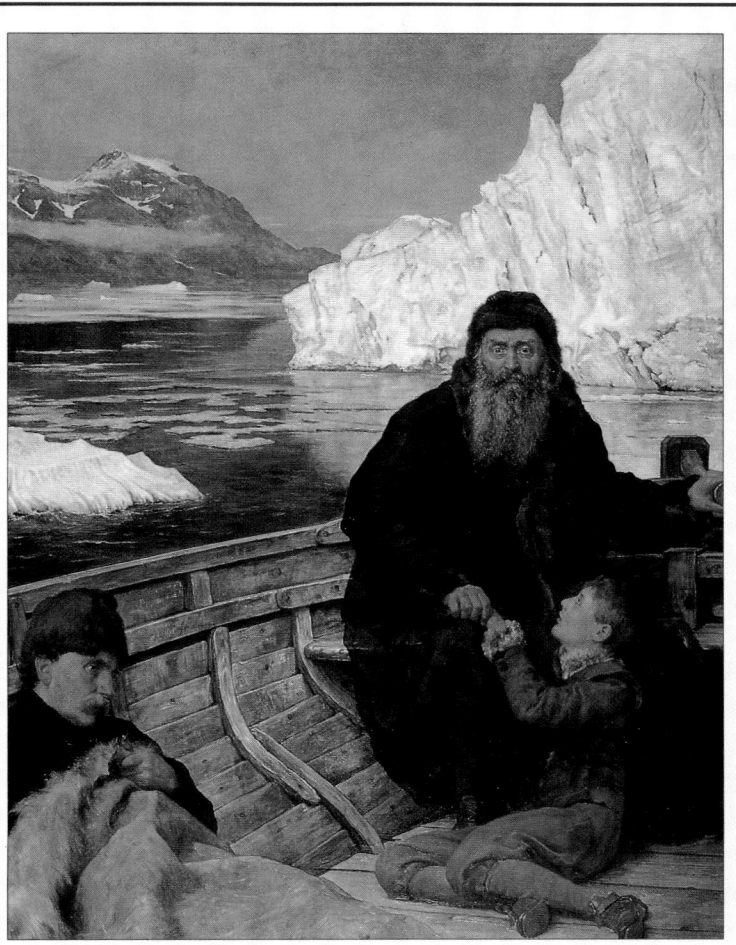

# WESTERN NORTH AMERICA

Once established in the Caribbean and Central America, the Spanish conquistadors spread out in all directions, including northward into North America.

The navigator Juan Ponce de Léon visited the coast of Florida in 1513. Spanish expeditions later pushed northward from Mexico by land and sea, still in search of Eldorado (see pages 62–63). Francisco Vásquez de Coronado reached as far north as modern Kansas in 1540–1542, while his colleague Garcia Lopez de Cárdenas reached the Grand Canyon in modern Arizona, in the west of the continent.

Meanwhile others explored the west coast. Francisco de Ulloa explored the Gulf of California in 1539–1540; Juan Rodríguez Cabrillo reached the site of modern San Francisco in 1543.

In the late 18th century the west coast of Canada was surveyed by several scientific expeditions, including those of Bruno de Heceta and Juan de la Bodega y Cuadra in 1775, and Alessandro Malaspina in 1791–1792. George Vancouver, who sailed with Captain Cook on his second and third voyages, was in the region at the same time, and claimed it for Britain.

By the end of the 18th century the east coast American states were pressing westward. The 19th century saw a concerted effort by the United States to map the West, which coincided with white settlement and increasingly bitter conflict with the Indians.

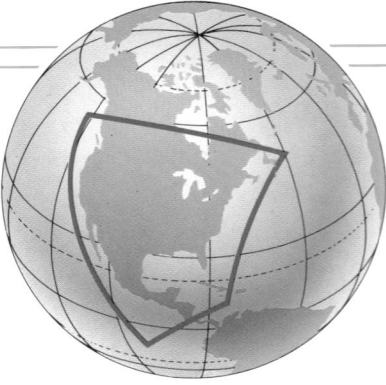

## The Louisiana Purchase

In 1803 the United States government purchased Louisiana — a huge tract of French territory in central North America. President Jefferson asked Meriwether Lewis, seen here in typical frontiersman garb, to lead a "Corps of Discovery" across the land to the Pacific — a journey that took almost 18 months to complete.

**Above** The Rocky Mountains, rising to over 13,000 feet (4,000m), form a natural barrier between the Great Plains of North America and the west coast. Until Lewis crossed them, the Rockies were known only to fur trappers — often French Canadians.

**Above** Spanish settlements in North America were pioneered by Juan de Oñate in 1598, and a Catholic mission was founded in Santa Fe in 1609. Others followed, spreading across the southwest.

**Left** The first white men to see the spectacular Grand Canyon were members of an expedition led by Garcia Lopez de Cárdenas in 1540. It was explored in 1776 by James O. Peattie, a fur trapper.

VANCOUVER ISLAND

Fort Clatsop

Snake

*Rocky Mountains*

Great
Salt
Lake

Missouri

Platte

Independence

St. Louis

Ohio

Arkansas

San Francisco

Grand
Canyon

*Colorado*

Santa Fe

Albuquerque

Rio Grande

Mississippi

ATLANTIC

OCEAN

PACIFIC

OCEAN

LOWER CALIFORNIA

El Paso
del Norte

SARGASSO
SEA

FLORIDA

BAHAMAS

GULF OF
MEXICO

Havana

CUBA

Tenochtitlán
(Mexico City)

Compostela

Acapulco

CARIBBEAN
SEA

→ Ponce de Léon (1513)

◂▸ Ulloa (1539-40)

◂▸ Coronado/Cárdenas (1540-42)

⇨ Cabrillo (1542-43)

➤ Oñate (1598-1605)

◂▸ Bodega y Cuadra (1779)

➤ Lewis (1804-05)

— Oregon Trail

French Louisiana

**Above** Up until the 19th century, European exploration in southern North America led directly to the division of the continent into three parts.

**Left** Mountain men such as John Moss, seen here with the Paiute Indian chief Tercherum, played an important part in opening up the West. The U.S. army used their specialized knowledge and friendships with local Indians to protect settlers, especially those who followed the Oregon Trail.

**Below** Trading posts such as Fort Laramie offered welcome protection to wagon trains from marauding Indians. Wagon trains carried settlers and their families who came in ever-increasing numbers, hoping to make their fortunes in the new lands of the American West.

The Aboriginals of Australia and the islanders of the South Pacific lived in comparative isolation for many thousands of years until the European explorers arrived.

## THE FIRST SETTLERS

The Aboriginals of Australia reached their continent some 50,000 years ago, probably by island-hopping from Southeast Asia, then walking from New Guinea when the sea level was lower than it is today. About 10,000 years ago the first occupants of the islands of the South Pacific sailed forth, also from Southeast Asia, to Melanesia. Polynesia was settled about 3,500 years ago, and Micronesia about 3,000 years ago. The Polynesians then spread out to reach New Zealand in about AD 950.

The skills of the Polynesian navigators allowed them to sail for many days out of sight of land, judging their position by the stars, the swell, and the flight of sea birds. Similarly, the Aboriginals knew their huge and often difficult terrain intimately. Routes called songlines led across the continent.

These societies had little to offer the rest of the world in terms of trade or gold. But they did have land, and this began to be taken from them by the Europeans in the 18th century.

Ownership of the land is still a matter of contention, particularly in New Zealand where many Maoris believe that the British failed to honor treaty obligations.

### Dreamtime

The Aboriginals of Australia believe that the world was created during Dreamtime, when giant animals with human characters shaped the world out of a grey, flat mass. The Aboriginal way of life and their code of behavior was also set out during Dreamtime and handed down through the generations. Most Aboriginal works of art, such as the intricately patterned bark-painting (right), relate to Dreamtime. The Aboriginal below is making a didgeridoo, a traditional wind instrument, the origins of which are lost in the mists of time. Aboriginal art and culture is much studied today by anthropologists.

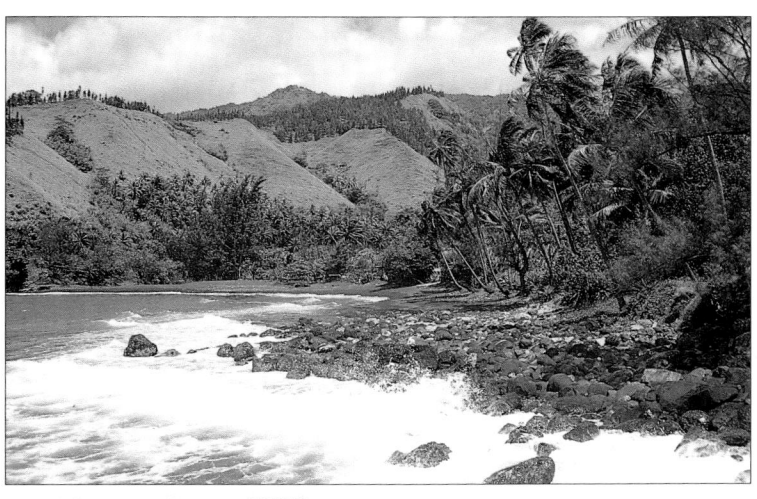

**Left** There are tens of thousands of islands such as Tahiti in the South Pacific, mostly lying within the Tropics.

**Below** The South Pacific islands were occupied by settlers originally from Southeast Asia, who arrived over a period of 10,000 years or more. For their part, the Aboriginals of Australia had occupied their land for 50,000 years before European arrival.

### They couldn't believe their eyes!

Much of the wildlife of Australia is unique. All but a few obscure marsupials (animals with pouches) come from this region, including the kangaroo, koala, and wombat. The egg-laying duck-billed platypus is so unusual that, when first shown a skin in 1797, scientists thought it was a hoax.

JAPAN

CHINA

Settlement of Melanesia c.10,000 years ago

Settlement of Micronesia 3000-2000 BC

Settlement and expansion of Polynesia 1000 BC-AD 1000

Explorers and settlers from Society Islands c. AD 1000

Explorers and settlers from Marquesas Islands before AD 500

HAWAIIAN ISLANDS

PHILIPPINE ISLANDS

MARIANA ISLANDS

WAKE ISLAND

M I C R O N E S I A

CAROLINE ISLANDS

MARSHALL ISLANDS

KIRIBATI (GILBERT ISLANDS)

LINE ISLANDS

FANNING ISLAND

BORNEO

INDONESIA

NEW GUINEA

NEW IRELAND

NEW BRITAIN

SOLOMON ISLANDS

M E L A N E S I A

VANUATU (NEW HEBRIDES)

FIJI

SAMOA

MARQUESAS ISLANDS

TUAMOTU ARCHIPELAGO

NEW CALEDONIA

TONGA

COOK ISLANDS

SOCIETY ISLANDS TAHITI

AUSTRAL ISLANDS

PITCAIRN ISLAND

EASTER ISLAND

AUSTRALIA

NORFOLK ISLAND

KERMADEC ISLANDS

P O L Y N E S I A

NORTH ISLAND

**NEW ZEALAND**

SOUTH ISLAND

CHATHAM ISLAND

### Maori culture

The Polynesians first settled in New Zealand (right) about 1,000 years ago. They called this land Aotearoa, and developed their own distinctive Maori culture, living by fishing and farming. They wore cloaks made of feathers, and the chieftains tatooed their faces with complex spiraling patterns.

# TERRA INCOGNITA AUSTRALIS

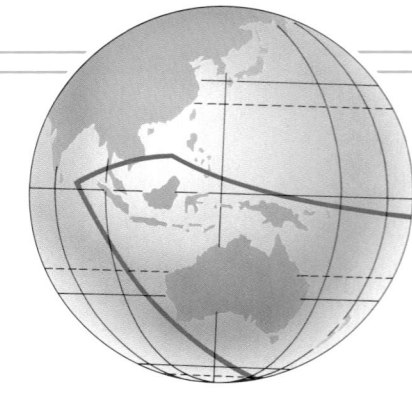

By the 1530s, European explorers had traveled to Africa, South America, and the Far East, but a major mystery still intrigued them. Where was the great southern continent shown on Ptolemy's map (see pages 10–11) and known as *Terra Australis*, "southern land?"

The Spanish conquistadors, believing Inca legends, hoped that such lands might contain rich new sources of gold as well as new territories to claim. They sent a number of expeditions to the South Pacific from the 1530s onward. In 1606 Fernandez de Quiros set out from Peru and found a new land, which he named La Austrialia del Espiritu Santo, but it was only an island of the New Hebrides (Vanuatu).

That same year the Dutchman Willem Jansz became the first recorded European to set eyes on Australia. He sailed into the Gulf of Carpentaria to make the first known European landing in Australia. The reconnaissance that followed culminated in the voyages of Abel Tasman. The Dutch were now the new power in the southern seas and had soon built a trading empire for themselves based in Batavia (Jakarta), founded in 1619.

**Below** People of Papua New Guinea. The name New Guinea reflected European dreams of finding gold in the South Pacific, just as it had been found in Guinea, West Africa. Such hopes were dashed.

Australia was named New Holland by the Dutch. The north and west coasts became fairly familiar to them over the next few decades, and the systematic voyages of Abel Tasman in the 1640s began to reveal the shape of these new lands. But trading opportunities seemed slim, and consequently the Dutch showed little interest in pursuing their discoveries.

**Left** This map of 1570 shows a huge southern continent attached to Tierra del Fuego, off the southern coast of South America. Here it is called *Terra Australis Nondum Cognita*, "southern land not yet discovered." Only the vague shape of northern Australia appears, based on reports by Portuguese navigators who followed in Magellan's wake after he had made the first crossing of the Pacific in 1520–1521.

## The Dutch East Indies

The Dutch adventure in Southeast Asia began in 1595 when Cornelis de Houtman sailed from the Netherlands to the South Seas with 249 men. Only 89 men returned, but their journey took them to the islands of Indonesia, including Java and Bali. Reports of these rich lands caused excitement in Amsterdam.

In 1602 the *Verenigde Oostindische Compagnie* (*VOC* — United East India Company) was formed and it soon took over most of the Portuguese trade in Indonesia. It became the world's most powerful trading organization.

→ Jansz (1605-06)

→ De Quiros (1606)

→ Tasman (1642-43)

→ Tasman (1644)

▦ Coast visited by the Dutch before Tasman

**Above** The history of the early exploration of Australia demonstrates the difficulties of mapping coasts and islands. Until every part of every coast is carefully examined, it is not clear which parts are attached to which others.

## Dutch Australasia

Abel Jansz Tasman (1603–1659) entered the service of the Dutch East India Company in 1632, and spent most of the rest of his life in the Far East. He led two major expeditions, in 1642 and 1644. The 1642 voyage proved that "New Holland" (Australia) was an island. It also made Tasman the first European to visit Aotearoa, which he renamed New Zealand. (Zeeland is a province of the Netherlands.)

Tasman's voyages made a major contribution to European knowledge of the region. His map of 1644, however, shows that his expedition of that year failed to grasp that New Guinea was a separate island. Also, Van Diemen's Land (Tasmania — right) is shown on his map as part of mainland Australia.

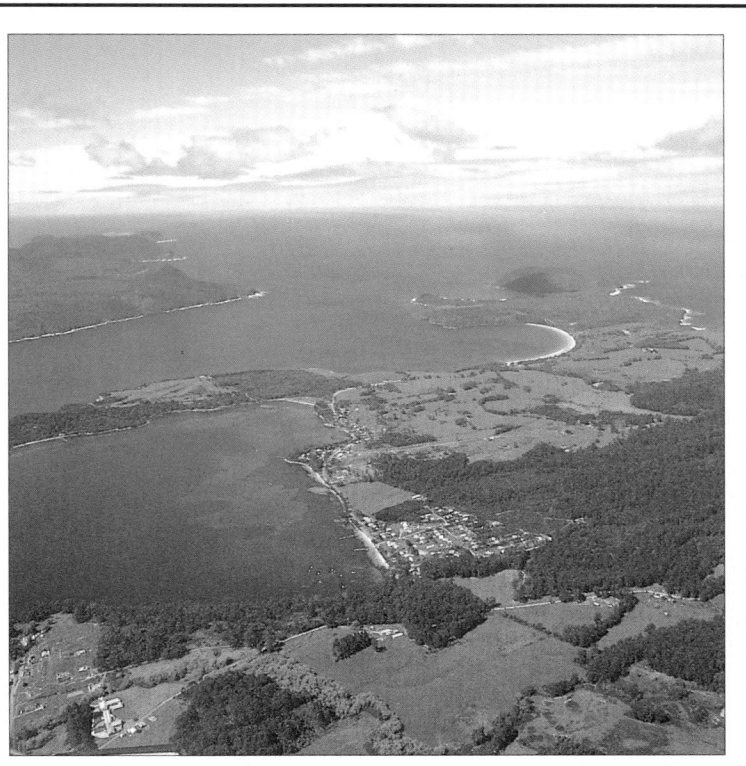

# CAPTAIN COOK

Over a century passed, and the huge territories visited by Abel Tasman in the 1640s remained virtually blank and unclaimed on the map even though much of the rest of the South Pacific was now being claimed by several European nations.

In 1768 James Cook (1728–1779) was appointed leader of a British naval expedition to the South Pacific to observe the passage of Venus between the Earth and the Sun. Cook, the son of a Yorkshire farm laborer, had risen rapidly through the naval ranks and was one of the first explorers to travel in the interests of knowledge and science. But he was also given secret instructions to locate *Terra Australis* once and for all, and to claim it for Great Britain. He sailed in the *Endeavour*, a coal ship specially fitted for surveying, and visited Tahiti, New Zealand, and Australia.

Two more expeditions followed. During the second voyage (1772–1775) he circumnavigated the world close to the Antarctic Circle, and established that no habitable continent existed south of Australia. In the third voyage (1776–1780) he set out to see if there was a western entrance to the Northwest Passage. It proved to be his last; he was killed in an incident on the Sandwich Islands (Hawaii).

**Left** Cook was an exceptionally gifted navigator, a kindhearted explorer, and a meticulous captain who cared deeply for the well-being of his crew.

**Above** Cook claimed Australia for Great Britain in April 1770 when he landed on an area of coast that now forms part of the suburbs of Sydney.

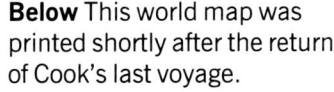

**Below** This world map was printed shortly after the return of Cook's last voyage.

## The Limeys

One of the great killers on any long voyage in Cook's day was a disease called scurvy, caused by a lack of vitamin C. Victims would suffer from terrible sores, lose their teeth, and waste away. Cook combated scurvy by insisting that his crew have as much fresh food as possible. In 1795 the British began to issue lime juice to their vessels which gave rise to the nickname "limey" for British sailors.

ASIA

BERING
SEA

Bering Strait

ALASKA

NORTH
AMERICA

CHINA

JAPAN

NORTH PACIFIC
OCEAN

GULF OF
ALASKA

Nootka Sound

MICRONESIA

SANDWICH ISLANDS
(HAWAIIAN ISLANDS)

HAWAII

GULF OF
MEXICO

BORNEO

Batavia
(Jakarta)

JAVA

NEW GUINEA

MELANESIA

POLYNESIA

INDIAN
OCEAN

NEW HOLLAND
(AUSTRALIA)

NEW
CALEDONIA

FIJI

TONGA

SOCIETY
ISLANDS

MARQUESAS
ISLANDS

TAHITI

TUAMOTU
ARCHIPELAGO

SOUTH
AMERICA

Botany
Bay

TASMAN
SEA

COOK
ISLANDS

EASTER
ISLAND

SOUTHERN
OCEAN

NORTH ISLAND

SOUTH ISLAND

NEW
ZEALAND

SOUTH PACIFIC
OCEAN

First expedition (1768-71)

Second expedition (1772-75)

Third expedition (1776-79)

Continuation of third expedition
after Cook's death (1779-80)

**Above** Cook's voyages
made the most thorough
examination of the Pacific up
until that time. With his skills
as a navigator, he fixed the
positions of many of the
islands for the first time.

**Above** Cook received a hostile
reception from the Maoris of
New Zealand when he first
reached their shores in 1769.
The highest mountain in New
Zealand still bears his name.

**Right** During Cook's third
voyage, a Sandwich islander
stole a boat, and Cook went to
investigate. The incident
turned into a violent dispute,
and Cook was killed.

# CROSSING AUSTRALIA

The settlement of Australia began in 1788 with the arrival of the first shipment of convicts from Britain, sentenced to transportation instead of prison. It continued with the foundation of coastal cities such as Sydney, Adelaide, Melbourne, and, in the west, Perth.

Matthew Flinders and George Bass had conducted extensive surveys of all the coasts by 1802, but the interior of Australia remained a mystery to all but the Aboriginals. Since rivers flowed inland from the coastal mountains, there was speculation that the middle of the continent might contain a vast sea, perhaps surrounded by fertile land. Charles Sturt failed to find this in his ventures inland from 1828 to 1846. Another explorer, Edward Eyre, had a similar disappointment in 1840 when he discovered only desert and salt flats.

Interest in the interior became more urgent with the coming of the telegraph and the need to lay long-distance cables. In 1859 the government of South Australia offered a prize to the first person to cross Australia south to north.

Robert O'Hara Burke and William Wills came tragically close to success in 1860–1861, but it was left to John McDouall Stuart to become the first to complete the journey the next year.

**Above** Those attempting to cross Australia from north to south had to travel over 1,250 miles (2,000 km) through rough terrain.

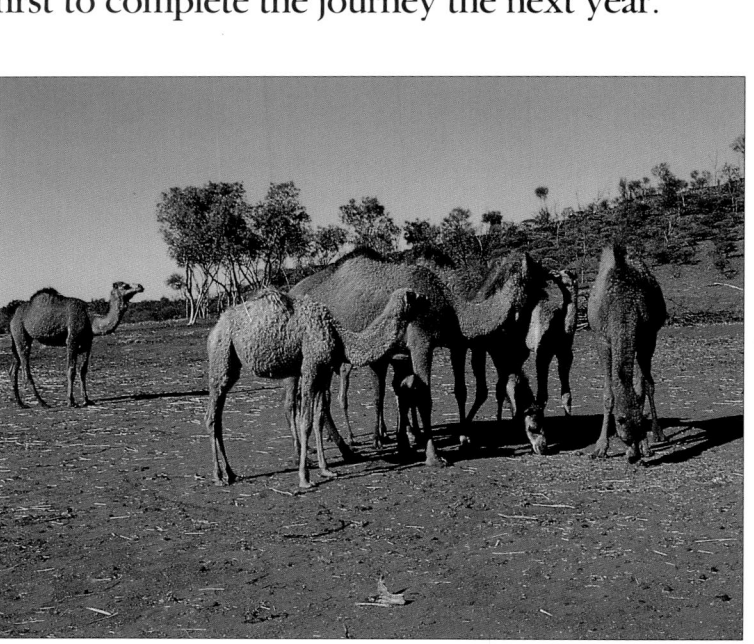

**Above** Burke and Wills were the first to see the merits of using imported camels in the interior of Australia. Camels later became widely used for carrying supplies and mail to remote farms and settlements. Their drivers were referred to generally as "Ghans," as many came from Afghanistan.

### Good grub

Burke and Wills perished where Aboriginals would have survived, and indeed it was Aboriginals who kept the explorers' only surviving colleague, John King, alive. Aboriginals have developed highly refined skills in hunting, knowing where water can be found, and using every possible form of food available. This includes a wide variety of wild fruits, seeds and roots, snakes and lizards, and insects and grubs, such as witchetty grubs (above). Their medicine also comes from wild plants and animals.

## First there and back

The first expedition to cross Australia from north to south successfully was led by John McDouall Stuart (1815–1866). He had migrated to Australia from Scotland in 1839, and had accompanied Sturt on an expedition into the interior in 1844, before turning to professional surveying. (His sextant is pictured, right.) He began a series of journeys into the heart of Australia in 1859, reaching its center in 1860, before making the complete crossing in 1861–1862.

**Right** Early settlements in Australia were dotted around the outskirts of the continent. The center is a vast desert, but this was not fully understood during most of the 19th century.

NEW GUINEA

JAVA

TIMOR

ARAFURA SEA

Torres Strait

Van Diemen Gulf

Darwin • **ARNHEM LAND**

Cape York

Gulf of Carpentaria

PACIFIC OCEAN

INDIAN OCEAN

• Tennant Creek

Great Sandy Desert

Great Dividing Range

Alice Springs

Gibson Desert

McDonnell Ranges

Simpson Desert

A U S T R A L I A

Brisbane •

Great Victoria Desert

**NEW SOUTH WALES**

Nullarbor Plain

Darling

Perth

Esperance

Great Australian Bight

Flinder's Range

Menindee •

Sydney •

Botany Bay

Albany

Port Lincoln

Spencer Gulf

Murray

Adelaide

Melbourne •

Bass Strait

**TASMANIA**

Hobart •

- ➡ Flinders (1798-99)
- ➡ Flinders (1802-03)
- ➡ Eyre (1840-41)
- ➡ Sturt (1844-45)
- ➡ Burke and Wills (1860-61)
- ➡ Stuart (1861-62)

## Tragic failure

Burke (1820–1861) and Wills (1834–1861) set out from Melbourne in August 1860. Their expedition soon began to break up. Burke, Wills, Charles Gray, and John King struck out alone from Cooper Creek, leaving William Brahe with the supplies . Burke and Wills reached the Gulf of Carpentaria, then rejoined Gray and King for the journey home. Gray died before they stumbled into Cooper Creek seven hours after Brahe had left. By the time the second of two search parties (imaginatively portrayed in the popular press, left) found them, only King was still alive.

# NEW ZEALAND AND THE PACIFIC ISLANDS

Although Abel Tasman had visited Australia and New Zealand in the 1640s, the European powers were slow to investigate the South Pacific. Over time, however, passing adventurers' enticing reports of these beautiful islands began to fire the European imagination.

In the latter part of the 18th century governments started to sponsor voyages of scientific exploration, such as the British naval expedition to the Pacific under John ("Foulweather Jack") Byron in 1764. In 1767, sailing in the same ship, Samuel Wallis became the first European to visit Tahiti. Cook's famous voyages took place between 1768 and 1780 (see pages 74–75). But as had happened elsewhere, exploration was followed by European claims to territory, especially from Britain and France. Both were eager to expand their empires.

This same process was slowed down, but not halted, in New Zealand with the arrival of missionaries in 1814. They had considerable success in converting the Maoris to Christianity, and explored much of the land with Maoris as their guides. Defending Maori interests, the missionaries opposed the idea of European settlement, but in 1840 the first 1,000 settlers arrived and colonization began — eventually at the expense of the Maoris.

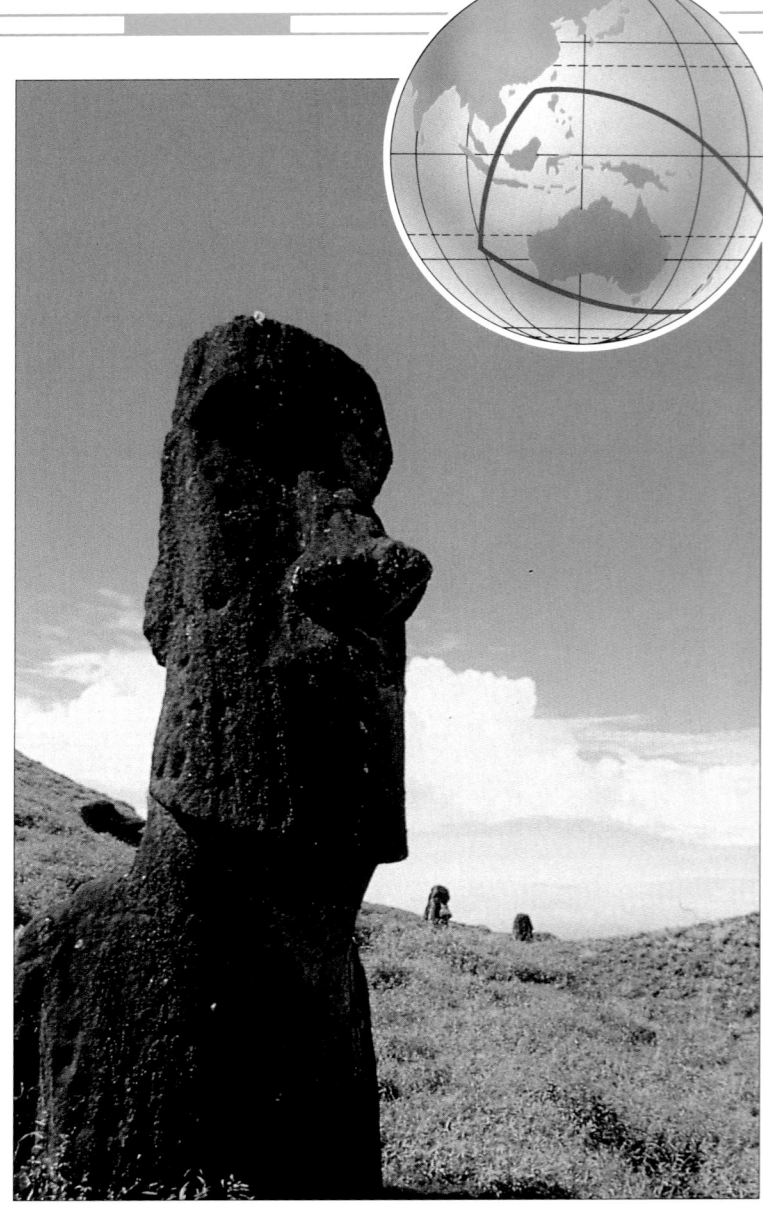

**Above** The Dutch admiral Jacob Roggeveen gave Easter Island its name because that was the day on which he reached it in 1722. Although it is set some distance from the main cluster of Polynesian islands, and 2,350 miles (3,780 km) from the South American coast, Polynesian settlers reached Easter Island in the distant past. About 1,000 years ago they carved over 600 enormous stone heads, some of which still remain. They are as tall as 65 feet (20 m) and weigh over 50 tons.

### The real Robinson Crusoe

William Dampier (1650–1715) was one of a number of daring and ruthless English adventurers who roamed the Caribbean and the Pacific during the late 18th century. He made his fame and fortune by raiding Spanish settlements on the west coast of South America in 1679. He then traveled west to New Holland (Australia) before completing his trip around the world.

Dampier would be seen as just another buccaneer if he had not had a more thoughtful side. A keen observer of everything that presented itself to him, he wrote a colorful account of his voyage under the title *A New Voyage Round the World*. Published in 1697, it became a bestseller, helping to ignite the public's interest in the South Seas.

In 1699 he was selected to lead an official naval expedition to the Pacific, during which he visited the west coast of Australia and discovered the island of New Britain. In 1703 he was back to buccaneering again. On this occasion one member of his crew, Alexander Selkirk, made himself so unpopular that Dampier abandoned him on the remote islands of Juan Fernández, 300 miles (485 km) off the coast of Chile.

Selkirk survived on the island for four years. After his rescue, he returned to Britain. The author Daniel Defoe heard his accounts of his adventures and used them to form the basis of his novel *Robinson Crusoe*, which was published in 1719 and which has been popular ever since!

CHINA

NORTH PACIFIC
OCEAN

NORTH
AMERICA

INDOCHINA

Saigon

SINGAPORE

Manila
PHILIPPINE
ISLANDS

SOUTH
CHINA
SEA

BORNEO

Batavia
(Jakarta)

NEW
GUINEA

NEW
BRITAIN

M E L A N E S I A

ESPIRITU SANTO

HAWAII

MARSHALL
ISLANDS

GILBERT ISLANDS
(KIRIBATI)

BYRON ISLAND
(NIKUNAU)

NAVIGATORS' ISLAND
(SAMOA)

SOCIETY ISLANDS

SOUTH
AMERICA

INDIAN
OCEAN

AUSTRALIA

VANUATU
(NEW HEBRIDES)

NEW CALEDONIA

FIJI

TONGA

P O L Y N E S I A

TAHITI

SOUTH PACIFIC
OCEAN

EASTER ISLAND

JUAN FERNÁNDEZ
ISLANDS

NEW ZEALAND

FALKLAND
ISLANDS

➡ Roggeveen (1721-22)

⇢ Tasman (1642-43)

➡ Byron (1764-66)

➡ Dampier (1699-1700)

➡ Bougainville (1767-68)

**Above** It was Cook who eventually brought systematic exploration to the South Pacific. It had been visited by a number of other explorers, but their varying accounts and inaccurate mapping often made it hard to find isolated islands a second time.

**Right** The geysers of New Zealand inspired the wonder of the early missionaries and settlers. The most famous are at Rotorua, but hot springs are scattered over some 5,000 square miles (13,000 sq km) of North Island.

## Empty promises

In about 1840 a rumor spread through Europe that the French intended to claim New Zealand for themselves. The British government, which had held back settlement on the islands for several decades, now felt obliged to act. A warship was dispatched with instructions to make a treaty with the Maoris.

The Treaty of Waitangi

was duly signed in 1840. The Maoris gave up sovereignty of their lands to Britain, but in return they were to have "full and exclusive possession of their lands and estates." This did not please the British settlers who had arrived in 1840. They pressed ahead with their claims to land despite the Treaty, triggering the Maori Wars that lasted from 1843 to 1872.

## Flower of French exploration

After the end of the Seven Years' War in Europe in 1763, naval ships were sent abroad on missions of scientific discovery. One, commanded by Count Louis Antoine de Bougainville, sailed on France's first circumnavigation in 1767–1769. He laid to rest the idea that Vanuatu was a part of *Terra Australis*. He is remembered by the name of a flower, the *bougainvillea*.

# SECTION 7: THE FINAL FRONTIERS

A century ago much of the world had been explored. But there were still places — the North and South poles, many mountain tops, the ocean depths — unvisited by humans. It took great courage and skill to reach these places and to confront the greatest challenge — space.

## THE NORTH POLE

The first attempts to reach the North Pole were part of the long series of expeditions to find the Northeast and Northwest Passages (see pages 34-35 and 66-67). A persistent theory suggested that the North Pole might be surrounded by open sea, and a route to the East might lie across it. In 1827 a British naval officer, William Edward Parry (1790-1855), attempted to reach the Pole in boats hauled over the ice.

By the 1880s it was clear that the Pole lay in the middle of a permanent ice cap. The race was on to see who could reach it using sleds and skis.

The winner was probably Robert Peary, an American, who claimed to have reached the Pole in 1909 with his black companion Matthew Henson and four Inuit (Eskimos). Peary was a coal engineer in the U.S. Navy. In 1884 he was posted to Central America to work on a canal project in Nicaragua. But Peary preferred the chill of the polar regions to the heat of the subtropics. In his boyhood he had

**Above** The Arctic, one of the most inhospitable places in the world, is also one of the most unpopulated. Apart from a handful of research scientists and Inuit who have settled in various places there since 3000 BC, the area is virtually uninhabited.

### Polar pioneer

In 1888, when he led an expedition across the Greenland ice sheet, Fridtjof Nansen (1861-1930) developed a sled based on the *komatik*, the traditional Eskimo sled.

To prove the theory that the icepack drifted eastward from Siberia to the North Atlantic, Nansen commissioned the *Fram*, a ship strong enough to withstand the ice. He sailed north of Siberia, where it became icebound. For three years it drifted westward while the crew carried out detailed research.

Its path did not cross the Pole as Nansen had hoped, so he and a colleague left the ship and traveled over the ice with dog-drawn sleds and kayaks. They came within 250 miles (402 km) of the pole — the farthest north anyone had been.

read about the adventures of Elisha Kent Kane, America's first polar hero. When he was sent back to the United States, polar exploration became his main interest, and in 1886 he made his first journey to Greenland.

Another American, Frederick Cook, created some bitterness when he claimed to have reached the Pole the year before. It was not until 1968 that the American Ralph Plaisted, using snow scooters, became the first person definitely to reach the North Pole by an overland route.

**Above** The American aviator Richard Evelyn Byrd (1888-1957) flew over the North Pole in 1926 from Spitzbergen. Three years later he flew over the South Pole.

**Left** By reaching the North Pole, Peary achieved something that explorers had been attempting for nearly 100 years. In 1926, Roald Amundsen and Umberto Nobile flew over the Pole in an airship. In 1968-1969 Wally Herbert followed virtually the same route in the other direction by land.

**Below** Robert Peary, seen here in 1906, led several expeditions to Greenland before making three attempts on the North Pole between 1898 and 1909.

Map labels:
NORTH PACIFIC OCEAN
NORTH AMERICA
ALASKA
Barrow
CHUKCHI SEA
BEAUFORT SEA
Bering Strait
EAST SIBERIAN SEA
NEW SIBERIAN ISLANDS
ARCTIC OCEAN
LAPTEV SEA
ASIA
Limit of polar ice cap
North Pole
ELLESMERE ISLAND
Baffin Bay
KARA SEA
Davis Strait
GREENLAND
SVALBARD (SPITZBERGEN)
BARENTS SEA
EUROPE
maximum limit of drift ice
NORWEGIAN SEA
NORWAY

Legend:
→ Nansen (1893-96)
--▶ Nansen's attempt to reach the North Pole (1895)
⇒ Peary (1909)
⇢ Peary (1906)
⇨ Byrd (1926)
➤ Amundsen (1926)
⇨ Herbert (1968-69)

### Dressed for the weather

Keeping warm is the key to survival in the Arctic. Early explorers wore thick jerseys and fur hats. Those who followed learned from the Inuit and adopted their seal-skin boots, long, hooded anoraks, and leather (or wooden) snow goggles to protect their eyes from the fierce glare of the snow.

Over the last 50 years, clothing for extreme polar conditions has become lighter and warmer thanks to the development of synthetic fibers.

# ANTARCTICA

The race for the South Pole began after Peary announced that he had reached the North Pole (see pages 80-81). Until then, various 19th-century explorers had reached the edges of Antarctica. At the beginning of the 20th century, they began to push into the interior of the continent.

Expeditions were mounted by Germans, Norwegians, Swedes, British, French, Japanese, and Australians, mostly using ships with reinforced hulls to reach the base camps from which they made overland journeys. Among them was Robert Falcon Scott (1868-1912) who made two Antarctic journeys from 1901 to 1912.

The race was won by Roald Amundsen (1872-1928), an experienced Norwegian explorer. He reached the Pole on December 14, 1911, beating Scott's British team by just one month.

Today, about 30 research stations continue the work of these explorers by studying the Antarctic's geology, climate, and fauna. Travel has become easier with the use of motorized snow vehicles and light aircraft: powerful ''sno-cats'' were used on Vivian Fuch's Trans-Antarctic expedition of 1957-1958.

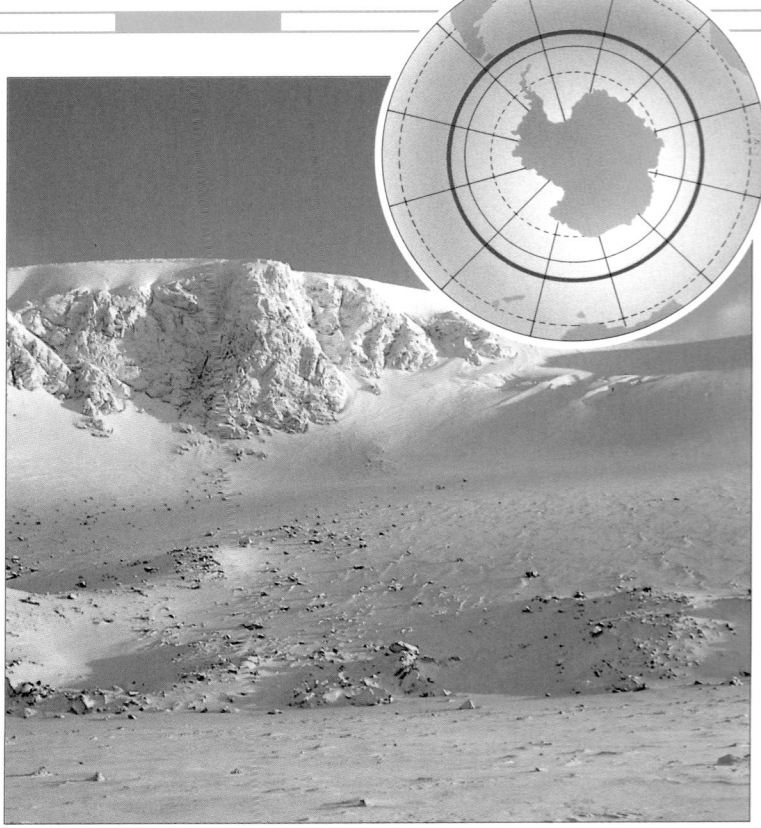

**Above** Unlike the Arctic, the Antarctic, which is a continent, is made of land covered with a layer of ice.

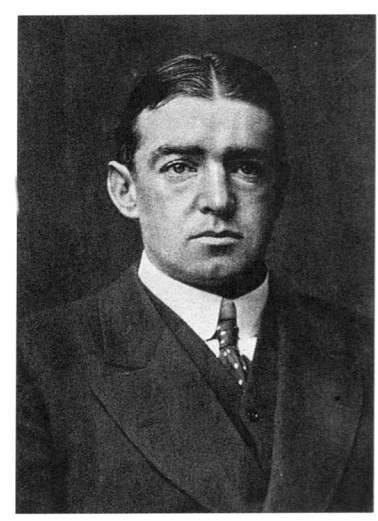

**Right** Ernest Shackleton (1874-1922) was one of the great Antarctic explorers. During his 1907-1909 expedition he came within 100 miles (160 km) of the Pole. He failed in his 1914-1917 expedition. In 1921 he set out on a third expedition but died in South Georgia a few months later.

## Into the unknown

After Cook's second voyage during which he sailed around the Antarctic (see pages 74-75), seal hunters sailed to the remote islands bordering the Antarctic. Few, however, ventured farther south.

Nonetheless, a growing scientific interest in the south polar region brought a series of navigators who began to chart its fringes. A Russian, Captain Fabian Gottlieb Bellingshausen, extended Cook's work by sailing around Antarctica in 1819-1821 and was probably the first to sight the Antarctic landmass. The British seal hunter Captain James Weddell charted the area around the Antarctic Peninsula in 1823.

Captain James Clark Ross (left) was the most experienced polar explorer of his day. He had been on several Arctic expeditions before leading the British navy's first major Antarctic expeditions in 1839–1843. He discovered the sea and ice-shelf now named after him.

Believing that the work involved in pulling a sled encouraged a sense of team spirit, his men (below), did not use dogs. This reluctance to use dogs had a decisive effect on the result of the final race for the South Pole. Captain Scott's team used ponies to pull their sleds. Too late, they realized that this was a mistake and shot the beasts before starting to haul the sleds themselves. Amundsen, who got to the Pole first, used dogs.

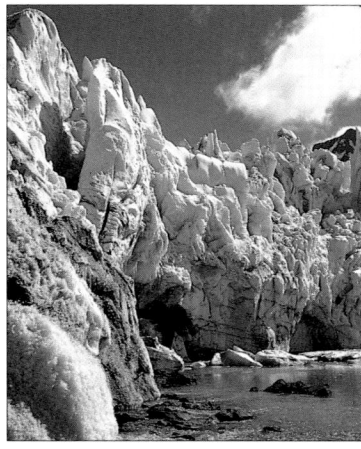

**Above** South Georgia. In 1914, after his ship, the *Endeavour*, was crushed by ice, Shackleton made a heroic 800-mile (1,280-km) journey in a small, open boat to this island.

## "I am just going outside . . ."

In October 1911, Captain Scott set out from his base camp with four companions: Lawrence Oates, Edward Wilson, Edgar Evans, and Henry Bowers. After an exhausting journey they reached the South Pole on January 17, 1912, but when they saw the tracks of Amundsen's team and the paw marks of his dogs, they realized they had been beaten to it.

Depressed, hungry, and suffering from scurvy, they began the long journey home. Evans died. Then, Oates became ill and, knowing he was holding the others up, he left the tent one night saying, "I am just going outside and may be some time." He walked to his death. Within a few weeks the others had also perished. Their frozen bodies, photographs, and journals were found by a search party eight months later.

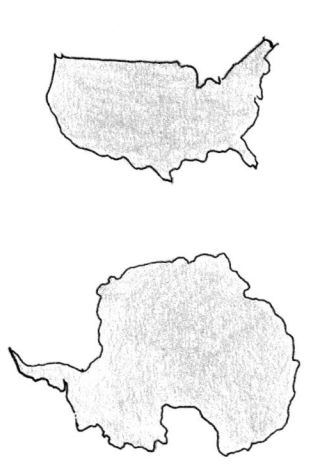

## A vast wasteland

At 5,400,000 square miles (14,000,000 sq km), Antarctica is larger than the entire United States of America. In winter, this area is extended by pack ice that forms when the seawater around the continent freezes. In several places flat areas of ice, called ice shelves, occupy the inner parts of the bays throughout the year.

Only in some parts of the Antarctic Peninsula are there areas where the land is exposed. The rest is permanently covered in ice.

➡ Shackleton (1908)

➡ Amundsen (1910-12)

➡ Scott (1910-12)

▪▪➤ Shackleton (1914-16)

*SOUTH ATLANTIC OCEAN*

PRINCESS MARTHA COAST

QUEEN MAUD LAND

*WEDDELL SEA*

LUITPOLD COAST

ENDERBY LAND

KEMP LAND

Antarctic Peninsula

Ronne Ice Shelf

South Polar Plateau

*BELLINGSHAUSEN SEA*

PRINCESS ELIZABETH LAND

▲ Mount Vinson

South Pole

*AMUNDSEN SEA*

**MARIE BYRD LAND**

WILHELM II LAND

Ross Ice Shelf

QUEEN MARY LAND

VICTORIA LAND

*ROSS SEA*

GEORGE V LAND

WILKES LAND

*SOUTHERN OCEAN*

**Above** Early attempts on the South Pole all began from the direction of the Ross Ice Shelf. Amundsen's route began from a point 60 miles (97 km) closer to the Pole than Scott's base camp.

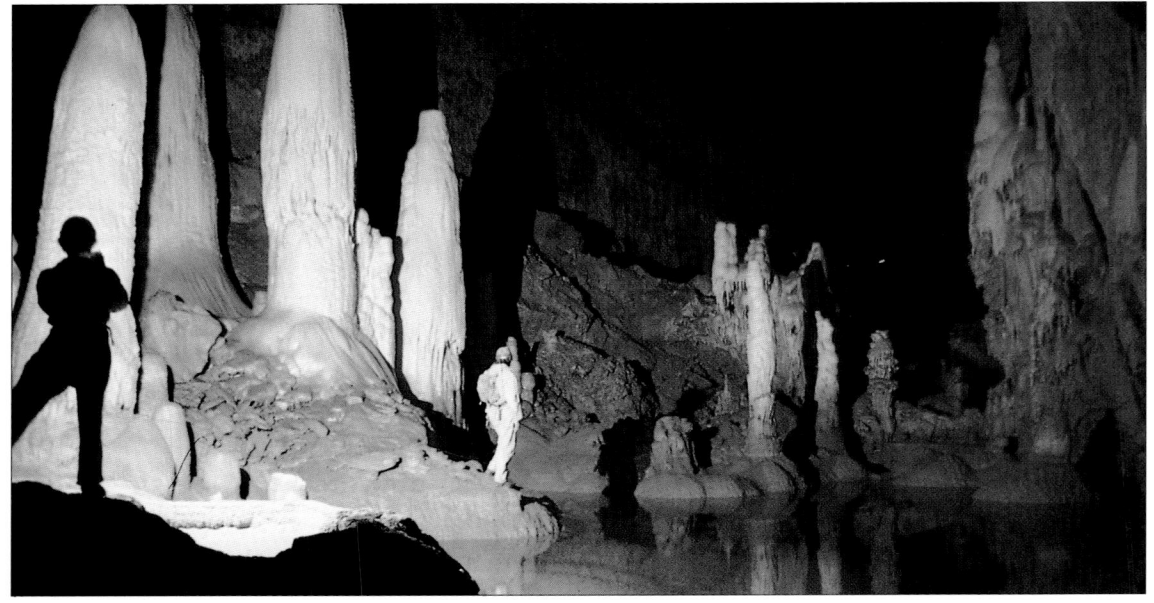

# MOUNTAINS AND CAVES

The father of modern mountain climbing was a Frenchman, Horace de Saussure (1740-1799). Before his time, only a few people had taken much interest in mountaineering. Saussure, an experienced climber himself, offered a prize to the first person to climb Mont Blanc in the French Alps. It was over 20 years before it was claimed — by Michel Paccard in 1786. By the late 19th century, mountain climbing had become a popular pursuit, and climbers were using increasingly sophisticated equipment to reach ever-higher peaks. Today, all the highest mountains of the world have been scaled, but numerous peaks and mountain faces still present new challenges for climbers, as does the choice of methods used.

It was a Frenchman, too, who popularized speleology — the exploration and study of cave systems. The discovery of prehistoric remains in caves during the 18th century had stimulated interest in caves, but it was not until the late 19th century that Edward Alfred Martel championed and popularized speleology — at first in Europe. Today, speleologists travel all over the world to explore underground caves and cave systems.

### On top of the world

Mount Everest, on the border between Nepal and China, was identified as the world's highest mountain in the 1850s.

There were at least eight failed attempts to conquer it before a carefully planned British expedition led by John Hunt set out in 1953.

With the help of Nepalese Sherpas as guides and porters, a series of camps was established on the mountain. The final stretch was climbed on May 29, 1953, by Edmund Hillary and Sherpa Tenzing.

Above The highest mountains in the world are all in the Himalayas. But height is not everything in the history of climbing. Each of the peaks here has represented a notable challenge within the various continents of the world.

## Mountain key

In just over 200 years, all the mountains in the map above have been climbed for the first time, as the list shows.

1 Mont Blanc (1786)
2 Matterhorn (1865)
3 Mt. Elbrus (1874)
4 Chimborazo (1880)
5 Kilimanjaro (1889)
6 Mt. Cook (1894)
7 Mt. St. Elias (1897)
8 Aconcagua (1897)
9 Mt. Kenya (1899)
10 Mt. McKinley (1913)
11 Mt. Logan (1925)
12 Communism Peak (1933)
13 Annapurna (1950)
14 Mt. Everest (1953)
15 Nanga Parbat (1953)
16 K2 (1954)
17 Kanchenjunga (1955)

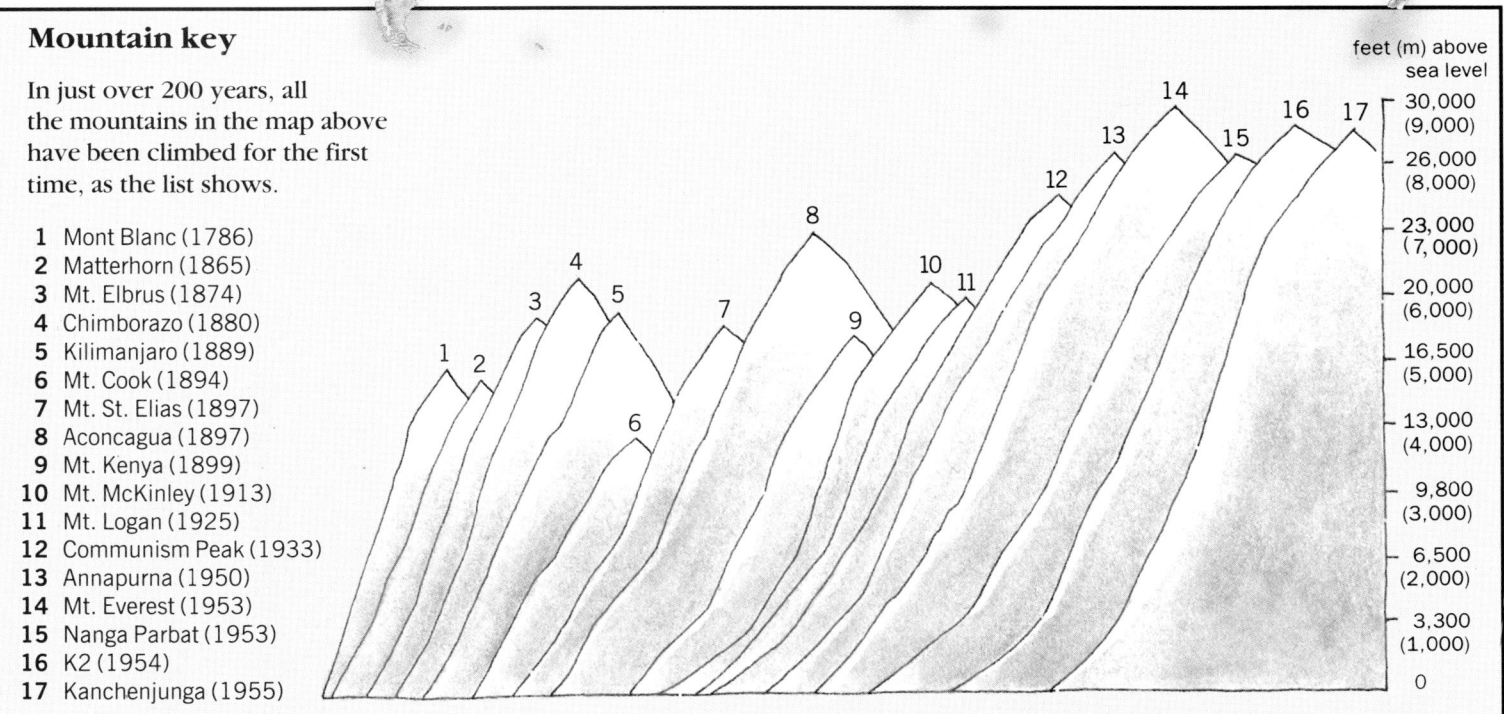

feet (m) above sea level
30,000 (9,000)
26,000 (8,000)
23,000 (7,000)
20,000 (6,000)
16,500 (5,000)
13,000 (4,000)
9,800 (3,000)
6,500 (2,000)
3,300 (1,000)
0

# UNDERWATER EXPLORATION

Until the 20th century, most of what was known about the sea had been learned from its surface. Surveyors on ships dropped lead weights on lines to measure the depth of the sea, and in the late 19th century scientists dredged up samples from the seabed and examined what they found. But they could not hope to have a complete picture until technological developments made it possible for them to see under water.

The first really efficient underwater breathing apparatus, the aqualung, was invented in the 1940s. Divers using aqualungs could descend up to 200 feet (61 m). This opened up a whole new world for exploration. From the 1930s on, special diving machines were constructed to withstand the immense pressures of the ocean depths. The American naturalist William Beebe (1877-1962) created the bathysphere, a small spherical vessel which was lowered on a cable from a ship to a depth of 3,032 feet (924 m) in 1934. Powered craft called submersibles, some operated by remote control, have since been developed and can explore the ocean floor to depths of 19,680 feet (6,000 m).

EUROPE

ASIA

AFRICA

Arabian Basin

*INDIAN OCEAN*

Mid-Indian Basin

West Australian Basin

Mid-Indian Rise

South Indian Basin

### A challenging expedition

The first major study of the oceans was undertaken by the British ship HMS *Challenger*, which circumnavigated the globe between 1872 and 1876. *Challenger* surveyed the complex topography beneath the waves for the companies laying submarine telegraph cables. The scientists on board also collected thousands of fish and plants.

Reports on the voyage took 25 years to complete and were published in 50 volumes, making an important contribution to the developing science of oceanography.

**Below** Diving bells were invented before diving suits and were used for such tasks as salvaging wrecks rather than for exploration. Once lowered into the water on a cable, they provided a bubble of air and dry, if cramped, working conditions for the operator. Edmund Halley's bell dates back to 1690. Fresh air was delivered to it in barrels.

Map labels:

ARCTIC OCEAN

Aleutian Trench

NORTH
AMERICA

North
Pacific
Basin

ATLANTIC OCEAN

EUROPE

North
American
Basin

PACIFIC OCEAN

AFRICA

Central
Pacific
Basin

East
Pacific Basin

Mid-Atlantic Ridge

Cape Verde Basin

SOUTH
AMERICA

Brazil Basin

East Pacific Rise

Walvis
Ridge

Southwest
Pacific Basin

Argentine Basin

IA

Pacific-Antarctic Ridge

ANTARCTICA

## Human gills

In 1825 William James developed the "self-contained underwater breathing apparatus" which we now call SCUBA. Controlling the supply of air remained a problem until 1865 when Benoit Rouquayrol and Auguste Denayrouze made a breakthrough with the discovery of the regulating valve. This allowed air to pass only when the divers breathed in. In 1943, Jacques Cousteau attached a regulating valve to a tank of liquid compressed air to make the aqualung used by SCUBA divers today.

## They came from under water

They may look like creatures from outer space, but they are, in fact, men wearing the diving suits of the 1840s and 1850s. The suits were made of thick waterproof canvas and the helmets of copper and glass. Air was supplied via tubes attached to a hand-pump on the surface.

The suits were worn by divers who needed to work under water and could be used only in shallow water.

**Above** A physical map of the ocean floor shows its complex terrain. It occupies more than seven tenths of the world's surface, but only a tiny portion of it has been fully explored.

**Below** The Swiss oceanographer Auguste Piccard (1884-1962) developed the bathyscaphe in the late 1940s. In 1960 a later version, the *Trieste,* was taken by his son, Jacques, to a depth of over 7 miles (11 km).

# INTO SPACE

People have always been fascinated by the heavens. The stars and planets have been the subject of intense study and speculation since ancient times and have played a central role in many religions. They have also played a vital part in the history of exploration.

However, the idea of exploring space remained totally impractical until the 20th century. German scientists developed a powerful rocket, the V-2, during the Second World War. Afterward, they helped both the Soviets and the Americans develop rockets powerful enough to reach the speed necessary for space flight, a colossal 17,500 miles (28,000 km) per hour.

On October 4, 1957, the former Soviet Union launched *Sputnik 1* the world's first artificial satellite — just 22 inches (56 cm) in diameter. It orbited the Earth in just 92 minutes. One month later, the dog Laika, aboard *Sputnik 2*, became the first living creature in space.

The United States launched its first satellite, *Explorer 1*, on January 31, 1958. Just over a decade later, on July 20, 1969, two Americans landed on the moon. They were the first of 12 Apollo astronauts to explore the lunar surface on foot in the greatest feat of exploration ever.

**Above** During medieval times, various ideas about the heavens were proposed. After the Renaissance, astronomers began to assemble accurate pictures of our solar system.

**Left** The American Robert Goddard, pictured on March 16, 1926, with his rocket, the first to use liquid fuel. He fired it successfully on a flight lasting 2.5 seconds.

**Below** The first stage in one of the greatest voyages of exploration. *Apollo 11*, with its three-man crew on board, blasts off from Cape Kennedy on July 16, 1969. Destination: the moon.

**Below** The Earth as seen from *Apollo 11* after it had gone into lunar orbit. The few men and women who have seen the Earth from space have all remarked on how beautiful it is. A few hours after this picture was taken, two of the astronauts prepared to clamber into the lunar module that would land them on the moon.

## The race to the moon

**Above** Yuri Gagarin, the first man in space, was ironically killed in a plane crash near Moscow in 1968.

**Below** John Glenn being helped into his space suit just a few hours before he became the first American in space.

On April 12, 1961, Yuri Gagarin became the first man in space. He orbited the Earth once in *Vostok 1* and returned after 108 minutes. John Glenn became the first American astronaut on February 20, 1962.

The Soviets moved ahead when they landed an unmanned spacecraft, *Luna 9*, on the moon in February 1966, a feat emulated by the Americans' *Surveyor 1* three months later.

The Americans pulled ahead with the launch of their *Apollo* missions.

**Below** The first woman in space was the Soviet, Valentina Tereshkova, in 1963.

## We have the technology . . .

The two Saturn rockets that launched the Apollo astronauts. Below is the 223-foot (68-m) high *Saturn IB*, which launched Apollo astronauts on test flights into Earth orbit. On the left is the mighty *Saturn V* rocket, which launched the astronauts to the moon. Standing 364 feet (111 m) high, it has a lift-off thrust of 3,500 tons — five times the power of the *Saturn IB*!

Command and service module (CSM)
Lunar module
Fuel tank
Third stage
Oxygen tank
Engine
Fuel tank
Second stage
Oxygen tank
Engine
Oxygen tank
First stage
Fuel tank
Engine

Command and service module (CSM)
Engine
Fairing
Fuel tank
Second stage
Oxygen tank
Engine
First stage
Engine

**Below** The *Apollo 11* lunar module, carrying Neil Armstrong and Edwin Aldrin, just after it has separated from the Apollo CSM mother ship. Michael Collins remains in the CSM as it continues in lunar orbit. Later it will rendezvous with the lunar module when that returns from the surface.

**Below** Edwin "Buzz" Aldrin climbs down the ladder of the *Apollo 11* lunar module to become the second man on the moon. The photographer, Neil Armstrong, had become the first human being to set foot on the moon a few minutes earlier. The historic date is July 20, 1969.

**Right** Mission complete, the *Apollo 11* lunar module prepares to dock in lunar orbit with the CSM.

**Below** Armstrong and Aldrin raise the Stars and Stripes as if to emphasize that the United States had clearly won the race to land men on the moon.

# JOURNEYS TO THE PLANETS

By the time the last of the Apollo moon landings took place, in December 1972, the next phase of space exploration was under way. It was the development of the space station, a large spacecraft in which astronauts could remain for long periods. The Soviet Union had launched its first space station, *Salyut 1*, in April 1971, but with little success.

In contrast, the first American space station, *Skylab* (launched May 1973), was a colossal success. Over a period of 10 months, three teams of astronauts lived on the station for longer and longer periods. The final crew stayed for 84 days, beating all space records. They proved that, properly equipped, human beings could survive in space for months.

In the 1980s Soviet cosmonauts repeatedly smashed the records, remaining in space for up to a year at a time in later *Salyuts*. Their current space station is called *Mir*.

After *Skylab*, the United States concentrated on developing the space shuttle. This is a reusable craft which takes off like a rocket, but

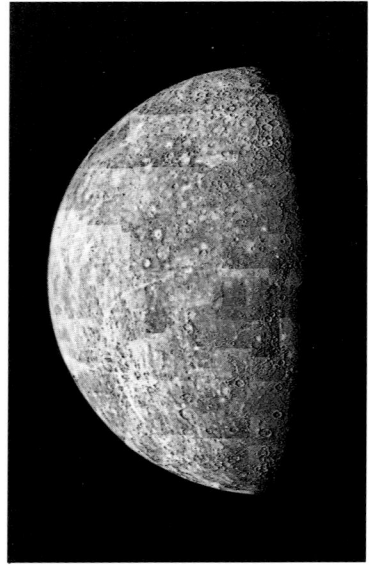

**Left** In 1974 and 1975, *Mariner 10* flew past Mercury three times and sent back thousands of close-up images. Scientists put them together to produce this picture of the second smallest planet in the solar system. It is not much bigger than our moon and, like the moon, it is pitted with craters.

lands on an ordinary runway like a plane. The first shuttle flight into space, by the orbiter *Columbia*, took place on April 12, 1981. Since then, there have been over 50 shuttle missions.

While manned spacecraft have been exploring space near the Earth, unmanned space probes have been exploring outer space. They have flown into the depths of our solar system, and visited all the planets except Pluto.

Plans are now being considered for the next great leap in space exploration, manned expeditions to the planets. Perhaps the history of exploration is only just beginning.

**Left** A montage of images of Jupiter and its four large moons, sent back by *Voyager 1* in 1979 when it passed within 175,000 miles (280,000 km) of the giant planet. The picture shows the planet at the top and, going clockwise from it, the moons Callisto, Ganymede, Europa, and Io.

**Below** This montage of *Voyager 1* pictures, taken in 1980, shows Saturn and some of its moons. The probe discovered many new moons and several new rings. All the rings proved to be made up of narrow ringlets, caused by light reflected from rocks whizzing around the planet at high speed.

PRELIMINARY TOPOGRAPHIC MAP OF VENUS

**Above** *Pioneer Venus* went into orbit around Venus in 1978. It used radar to penetrate the thick clouds and produce images such as this.

**Right** With all engines blazing, the space shuttle orbiter *Atlantis* blasts off the launch pad at the Kennedy Space Center in Florida.

**Left** Mars, viewed by an approaching *Viking* space probe in 1976. Pictures taken by the two *Viking* landers reveal that Mars gets its color from the red soil that covers most of its surface.

## Now Voyager

In 1977, the United States launched two *Voyager* probes. Both visited Jupiter and Saturn, and *Voyager 2* went on to Uranus and Neptune. *Voyager 2* reached Neptune in 1989. It arrived right on schedule after a journey of 12 years and 4,400,000,000 miles (7,000,000,000 km)!

The *Voyager* probes made many discoveries and sent back thousands of pictures. They discovered active volcanoes on Jupiter's moon Io; winds on Saturn blowing at 1,100 miles (1,800 km) per hour; chaotic landscapes on Uranus's moon Miranda; and liquid gas geysers on Neptune's moon Triton.

**Left** *Voyager 2* at Uranus in 1986. This picture montage shows the planet (background) and Miranda, one of its moons.

**Right** When *Voyager 2* flew past Neptune in 1989, it discovered that the planet is blue — due to the gases in its atmosphere.

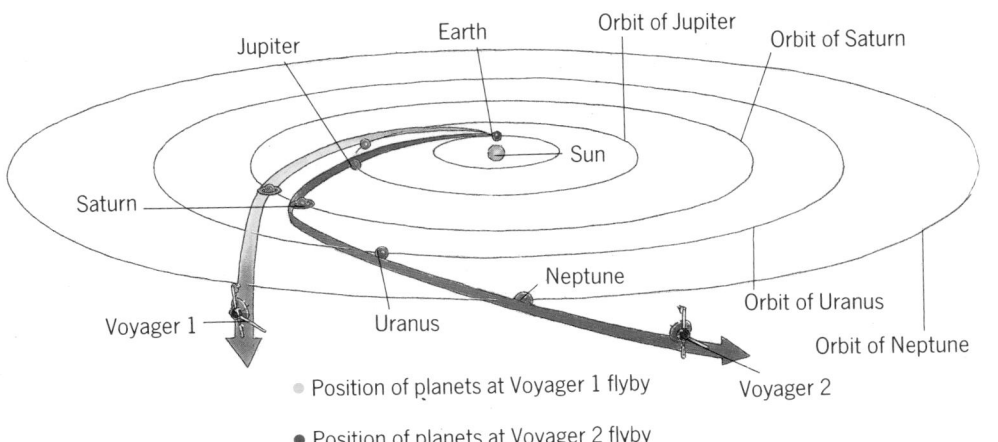

Jupiter  Earth  Orbit of Jupiter  Orbit of Saturn

Saturn  Sun

Neptune

Voyager 1  Uranus  Orbit of Uranus

Orbit of Neptune

Voyager 2

● Position of planets at Voyager 1 flyby

● Position of planets at Voyager 2 flyby

# TIME CHART

This time chart shows the landmarks of exploration (highlighted in green), and how they relate to the major events in world history. A glance at the time spans that separate the dates reveals how the pace of exploration accelerated rapidly during the 15th and 16th centuries and continued to increase from then on.

c. stands for circa, meaning about. It is used before dates which are approximate.

## BC

| | |
|---|---|
| c.9000 | *The beginnings of farming in Asia* |
| c.8350 | *The foundation of Jericho, the first walled city* |
| c.3000 | *The growth of the first great cities in Asia* |
| | *Early forms of writing develop* |
| c.2600 | *The Great Pyramid built at Giza* |
| **c.2300** | Harkhuf's expeditions up the River Nile |
| c.2000 | *The rise of Minoan civilization* |
| c.1700 | *The beginnings of Chinese civilization* |
| c.1500 | *The growth of the Hindu religion* |
| **1492** | Queen Hatshepsut's expedition to the Land of Punt |
| c.1000 | *Town-building civilizations develop in Central America* |
| 814 | *The Phoenicians found Carthage* |
| c.753 | *The foundation of Rome* |
| **c.600** | Pharaoh Necho's expedition circumnavigates Africa |
| c.563 | *The birth of Buddha* |
| **334-323** | Alexander the Great's expeditions in Asia |
| c.300 | *The early settlement of Polynesia* |
| c.221 | *The Great Wall of China developed* |
| 146 | *The Greek world falls to the Romans* |
| **138** | The voyage of Chang Chi'en to Central Asia |
| **c.100** | The development of the Silk Road across Asia |

## AD

| | |
|---|---|
| c.30 | *The death of Jesus Christ* |
| **127-150** | Ptolemy working at the Library of Alexandria |
| 391 | *Christianity becomes the official religion of the Roman Empire* |
| c.432 | *St. Patrick brings Christianity to Ireland* |
| 476 | *Collapse of the Roman Empire* |
| c.570-632 | *The life of the Prophet Muhammad* |
| **629-645** | The voyage of Hsüan Tsang in Asia |
| 711 | *The Muslim invasion of Spain* |
| 793 | *Viking raids on Europe begin* |
| c.900 | *The collapse of the Mayan civilization* |
| c.950 | *Maoris settle in New Zealand* |
| **1000** | Leif Eriksson reaches North America |
| 1096 | *The First Crusade* |
| 1206 | *The beginning of the Mongol conquest of Asia* |
| **1271-1295** | Marco Polo's travels in Asia |
| c.1325 | *The rise of the Aztec Empire* |
| **1325-1354** | Ibn Battuta's travels in Africa and Asia |
| 1348 | *The Black Death devastates Europe* |
| c.1350-1600 | *The Renaissance in Europe* |

### 1400

| | |
|---|---|
| c.1400 | *The rise of the Inca Empire* |
| **1405-1433** | Cheng Ho's naval expeditions, reaching Africa |
| **1434** | The beginnings of Portuguese exploration of West Africa under Henry the Navigator |
| 1445 | *Gutenberg's Bible, Europe's first printed book, is produced* |
| 1453 | *Ottoman Turks capture Constantinople* |
| **1487** | Pedro da Covilhã reaches India overland |
| | Bartolomeu Dias rounds the Cape of Good Hope |
| **1492** | Columbus reaches the Caribbean islands |

| | |
|---|---|
| 1494 | The Treaty of Tordesillas divides the New World between Portugal and Spain |
| 1497 | John Cabot reaches Newfoundland |
| 1498 | Vasco da Gama reaches India by sea |
| **1499-1502** | Amerigo Vespucci's expeditions to South America |

### 1500

| | |
|---|---|
| **1500** | Pedro Cabral reaches Brazil |
| 1510 | *The first African slaves are taken to the Caribbean* |
| **1512** | The Portuguese reach the Spice Islands |
| **1513** | Vasco de Balboa crosses Central America |
| | Juan Ponce de Léon reaches Florida |
| **1517** | Fernandez de Córdoba reaches Mexico |
| | *Martin Luther initiates the Reformation* |
| **1519-1522** | Ferdinand Magellan's expedition completes the first circumnavigation of the globe |
| **1521** | Hernán Cortés conquers the Aztecs |
| **1532** | Francisco Pizarro conquers the Incas |
| **1534** | Jacques Cartier sails up the St. Lawrence River |
| **1540-1542** | Francisco Vásquez de Coronado and Garcia Lopez de Cárdenas explore southwest of North America |
| **1542** | Francisco de Orellana travels down the Amazon |
| **1543** | Juan Rodriguéz Cabrillo sails up the southwest coast of North America |
| **1549** | St. Francis Xavier visits Japan |
| 1571 | *The Spanish conquest of the Philippines* |
| **1577-1580** | Francis Drake completes the second circumnavigation of the globe |

| | | |
|---|---|---|
| 1595 | *The Dutch begin trading in Southeast Asia* | |
| **1597** | Willem Barents dies trying to find a Northeast Passage | |

## 1600

| | |
|---|---|
| **1606** | Willem Jansz reaches Australia |
| 1608 | *The foundation of Quebec* |
| 1609 | *The invention of the telescope* |
| **1611** | The death of Henry Hudson |
| 1620 | *The Pilgrim Fathers land in New England* |
| 1624 | *New York founded by the Dutch* |
| 1639 (-1853) | *Japan is closed off to the world* |
| **1642-1644** | Abel Tasman's voyages around Australia and to New Zealand |
| 1648 | *The Taj Mahal is built in India* |
| **1679-1682** | Robert de La Salle travels down the Mississippi to the Gulf of Mexico |

## 1700

| | |
|---|---|
| **1728** | Vitus Bering sails through the Bering Strait |
| 1759 | *The conquest of Quebec by the British* |
| **1768** | James Bruce reaches the source of the Blue Nile |
| **1768-1779** | James Cook's three voyages in the Pacific and southern oceans |
| 1776 | *The American Declaration of Independence* |
| **1786** | Michel Paccard climbs Mont Blanc |
| 1788 | *The first settlements in Australia* |
| 1789 | *The French Revolution* |
| **1792-1793** | Alexander Mackenzie crosses North America |
| **1795-1806** | Mungo Park's expeditions in West Africa |
| **1799-1804** | Alexander von Humboldt's travels in South America |

## 1800

| | |
|---|---|
| 1803 | *United States buys Louisiana from France* |
| **1804-1806** | Meriwether Lewis and William Clark cross North America from St. Louis to the west coast |
| **1811** | Thomas Manning reaches Lhasa |
| 1815 | *The defeat of Napoleon at Waterloo* |
| 1825 | *The opening of the first passenger railway, in northern England* |
| **1828** | René Caillié reaches Timbuktu |
| **1831-1836** | Charles Darwin's voyage on HMS *Beagle* |
| 1837-1901 | *The reign of Queen Victoria in Great Britain and Ireland* |
| **1849-1855** | Heinrich Barth crosses the Sahara |
| **1853-1856** | David Livingstone crosses Africa |
| 1857-1858 | *The Indian Mutiny* |
| **1858** | John Speke reaches Lake Victoria |
| **1861** | Robert Burke and William Wills die while trying to cross Australia |
| **1861-1862** | John Stuart successfully crosses Australia |
| 1861-1865 | *The American Civil War* |
| **1864** | Samuel and Florence Baker reach Lake Albert |
| **1871** | Henry Stanley finds Livingstone |
| **1874** | Stanley proves that Lake Victoria is the source of the Nile |
| 1876 | *The invention of the telephone* |
| **1878-1879** | Adolf Nordenkiöld sails the Northeast Passage |
| **1895** | Mary Kingsley's travels in the French Congo |
| | *The invention of radio* |

## 1900

| | |
|---|---|
| 1903 | *The first successful powered flight, by the Wright Brothers* |
| **1903-1906** | Roald Amundsen sails the Northwest Passage |
| **1909** | Robert Peary reaches the North Pole |
| **1911** | Roald Amundsen reaches the South Pole |
| | Machu Picchu discovered |
| 1914-1918 | *The First World War* |
| 1917 | *The Russian Revolution* |
| **1924** | Alexandra David-Néel reaches Lhasa |
| **1930-1931** | Bertram Thomas crosses the Empty Quarter of Arabia |
| 1939-1945 | *The Second World War* |
| **1953** | John Hunt's expedition conquers Mt. Everest |
| **1960** | Jacques Piccard reaches the deepest part of the world's ocean floor in the bathyscape *Trieste* |
| **1961** | Yuri Gagarin becomes the first man in space |
| **1969** | Neil Armstrong and Edwin "Buzz" Aldrin become the first men on the Moon |
| **1989** | *Voyager 2* reaches Neptune |

# INDEX

# ACKNOWLEDGEMENTS

Quarto would like to thank the following for providing photographs, and for granting permission to reproduce copyright material:

Aker/Turner: 61a; Janet and Colin Bord: 14a; Nick Buzzard: 62b, 68b; Cambridge University Library: 44b; Jean-Loup Charmet: 7cr, 9al, 10bl, 12b, 15ar, 20bl, 25bl, 27a, 32bl, 53ac, 87bl; Anthony R. Dalton: 17ar; CM Dixon: 10ar, 12a, 13bl, 13br, 15al, 16bl, 16cr, 17br, 20br, 21cl, 23al, 23bl, 26a, 30c, 39c, 40b, 46bl, 63a, 66c, 70br; ET Archive: 6r, 7b, 8a, 8bl, 18a, 19b, 21br, 27b, 28c, 29b, 36a, 37c, 42b, 45c, 46br, 54a, 55a, 56c, 58bl, 62a, 63c, 65a, 66a, 67b, 71bl, 72b, 74b, 75br, 77a, 77b, 78b, 81a; The Fortean Picture Library: 7al, 33br, 78a; Leslie Garland Picture Library: 13a; The Hulton Picture Company: 84b; The Hutchison Library: 6l, 8br, 25br, 30a, 44a, 45b, 50b, 84c, 85a, John Dowman 55b, John Hatt 54br, Michael Macintyre 87cr, Bruce Wills 11c; Life File: Dr. R. Cannon 82a, Cliff Threadgold 23br; The Mansell Collection: 10br, 14b, 30b, 31a, 34c, 34b, 41b, 47br, 51a, 51b, 59b, 73bl, 86bl, 88a; NASA: 9ar, 88bl, 88br, 89cl, 89cr, 89bl, 89bc, 89br; National Maritime Museum: 35b, 58c; Peter Newark's Historical Pictures: 7ar, 24a, 48b, 49b, 52b, 53bl, 55c, 56b, 57a, 60b, 61b, 64b, 66b, 68al, 68c, 69bl, 69br, 74a, 81b, 82c, 82bl, 82br, 83ar, 86br, 87br; Panos Pictures: Alain Le Garsmeur 17c, 32ar, Ron Giling 43a, Neil Munns 42a, Bruce Paton 49b, David Reed 38c, 39b, Penny Tweedie 70bl; Quarto: 62c; Spacecharts: 88c, 89a, 89cl, 90a, 90bl, 90br, 91al, 91ar, 91cl, 91bl, 91br; Andrew Stewart: 40c, 41a, 50c; Trip: 47bl, 68ar, 80, 83al, Joan Batten 24bl, 52a, Colin J Conway 72a, Ian Fairweather 18br, Linda Jackson 32bl, Alexander Kuznetsov 34a, Bruce Low 71br, 72c, 79cr, Fiona Potter 64a, Richard Powers 58br, Helene Rogers 16br, 22b, 31b, 36b, 37a, 37b, 39a, 53ar, 56a, 57b, 75bl, Thelma Sanders 43b, 48a, 49a, Peter Saunders 26b, 42c, 46a, 63b, 71a, Joan Wakelin 73br, 76a, 76b, 79cl, Julia Waterlow 21bl; Michael Turner: 60a; Tony Waltham: 22a, 28a, 33a, 84a.

(a = above, b = bottom, c = center, l = left, r = right)

While every effort has been made to trace and acknowledge all copyright holders, we would like to apologize should any omissions have been made.